FORGOTTEN

Book 3 of the FADE Series™

By

Kailin Gow

FORGOTTEN: FADE Book 3

Published by Sparklesoup Inc.

First Published 2012

Copyright © 2012 by Kailin Gow

For information, please contact:

Sparklesoup.com

First Edition

Printed in the United States of America

ISBN: 978-1-59748-009-3

Kailin Gow

Henceforth space by itself, and time by itself, are doomed to fade away into mere shadows, and only a kind of union of the two will preserve an independent reality. – Hermann Minkowski

ONE

I'm drifting, floating in a way I know can't be real. Floating above a woman I know as well as anyone on the planet, for the simple reason that she's me. Celestra Caine. She has the same flowing dark hair falling past her shoulders, the same flawless skin and fine boned features, the same athletic frame. She's... *I'm* wearing a dark suit that's cut perfectly for me. There's a man beside me, wearing an almost identical suit. That's the most I can make out of him. My eyes seem to slide from his features every time I look at them. Along with the floating, that tells me that this is just a dream. That it isn't real. Yet somehow, I know that it is, or will be, or has been. I'm not sure which.

I'm not floating any longer. I'm looking out through her eyes. My eyes. It's so bright that I reach for a pair of shades automatically, the filtered lenses of them giving the world a darker cast. The field has changed a lot from the way it would have been back when it was in use. The whole climate is different now. The subsoil samples taken so far at the dig have proved that. Open trenches mark where the archaeological work has been taking place, mounds of soil beside them. With the way the open fields are now, it's hard to believe that this was once a desert.

I hop down into the nearest trench to get a closer look. It's a deep trench, and I have to climb down almost ten feet before I reach the bottom. There are flashes of metal there. It's still bright, despite the long years underground.

"Data drives?" the man with me asks, sounding a little surprised. "I know we've recovered some readable ones before."

"Possibly," I say. "The metals they used in these facilities protected them in a way most archaeological deposits from that time weren't protected. Even with that though, there's still a chance that they could have all degraded."

"Well, I guess a few thousand years in the ground will do that," the man replies. I can hear the tension in his voice though. We need this. "What else have you got down there, anyway?"

Taking a sonic brush from my pocket, I start to peel away the layers of dirt, very carefully, the ultra-sonic sound waves scraping it away more gently than a normal digging tool ever could. As he just said, these things have been in the ground for thousands of years.

"A lot of it looks like fairly standard lab equipment," I say, "though the typology seems a little off. Some of these things are more advanced than I'd expect given the period." It's hard to keep a note of excitement out of my voice. We both know what that is likely to mean.

"Keep going," my companion says, though he makes no move to join me in the trench. Probably he doesn't want to get his suit dirty, though I know for a fact he's gotten more on it than dirt before now. A lot more.

I keep rooting through the finds, hoping for something clear. Something definite. I sift through the soil, looking for things below the current layer of the trench. It's bad archaeology, when we haven't recorded everything at that level, but some things are more important. The fate of the world, for one.

What I find is a scrap of metal, a plate obviously designed to be bolted onto something else, but loose now. I pull it from the dirt and set about cleaning it carefully. If this place is what we think it might be, then the metals in it won't have corroded the way iron or even steel would have after all this time. It has just two words written on it, raised slightly from the surface so that as I run my hand over them, I can feel them.

Location Six.

"Do we know anything about a 'Location Six'?" I call up to the top of the trench. The man there nods, though I still can't seem to make out his features. The dream, or my memory, won't let me have that.

"It used to be a base belonging to the Underground. It's mentioned in some of the old records." He's trying not to sound too excited about it, but I can tell that he is from the slightly too rapid way he says that. Location Six is obviously a big deal. "I never thought that we'd actually find it."

"And now we have," I say. "You're going to have to bring in a team to collect the important parts from here."

He nods and takes an in-ear phone from a pocket, putting it in place and relaying details of the location. I notice that he doesn't tell the crew on the other end exactly what we have found. It's a very big deal, then.

For now though, I'm too busy climbing out of the trench to worry about that. Near the top, he reaches out for me, helping me from the trench with strong hands on mine. Immediately, and perhaps inevitably, he pulls me closer, one arm going around my waist. Even though he hasn't been in the trench, he has been standing around at the dig, and right then he smells earthy and solid.

I pull away anyway. "There isn't time."

"Make time."

I shake my head. "We aren't kids anymore, and this is too important to mess up by wasting time."

"Would it be a waste?"

"When there's so much at stake, yes." I look back down at the trench, away from him. "There's so little time left. All that down there might be the past, but it's also the key to the future. If we get things wrong, even a little, everything around you will vanish like it never existed."

"And you can't allow that."

I shake my head. "I can't. I won't. There are some things that it is worth taking risks to protect. It all means too much. Too much for us now. Too much for the future. Too much for *everything*."

I can hear the strength of the passion in my own voice, and in that moment I know how important what we are doing is, but I can't quite remember why. I can't quite focus. I'm drifting too much. Drifting, and listening to the voice I can hear on the edge of my thoughts, calling my name.

"Celes. Celes, come on. Wake up."

TWO

"Celes, wake up."

My eyes blink their way open and I find myself looking up at Jack Simple's face. There are definitely worse things to look at in the world when waking up. His dark hair is short and normally stylishly arranged, though now it's a mess. There's a light dusting of stubble over his features, which is strange, because normally they're clean shaven for an elegantly suave look. I have to admit it suits him though. It even goes with the combat gear he's wearing, left over from our rescue mission into the Others' base.

The look in those icy blue eyes of his is one of worry as I start to sit up on the low bed I'm currently lying on.

"How are you feeling, Celes? Are you okay?" His delicately British accent normally doesn't give much away, but right now I can hear the concern there. Like he's afraid I shouldn't be standing up.

"I'm fine, I think." I stand up carefully. My legs are a little shaky, but I'm quickly on my feet. I'm still dressed the way I was the last I remember, in camouflage combat gear that matches Jack's. More of those memories come back to me.

"Lionel drugged us."

Jack nods. "He must have found out what happened."

What happened was that I killed a member of the Underground in self-defense, the organization for which Jack works, and in which Lionel is one of the most senior figures. Not to mention very dangerous for someone who looks like he could be somebody's grandfather, with his silver hair and twinkling eyes. It turns out that he doesn't like people who don't match his idea of human very much, or at least doesn't trust them.

That means people like me, since I can do so many things that normal humans can't do. Things like burning one of his agents with a power that seems to almost have a mind of its own. It means people like Jack too, though Lionel has only just found that out. Maybe that's why we're here. Wherever here is.

More likely it has something to do with the part where I was trying to get as far away from him and his faction of the Underground as possible. As far as I can tell, they aren't much better than the Others, the group that wants to kill all those like me. One of Lionel's people found me sneaking out, and I ended up burning him up. But only after he tried to kill me. It seems my ability to burn mostly comes up when I'm scared or trying to defend myself or someone I cared about...like an adrenaline rush.

I look around the room Jack and I are in. It's very white. White as in the white of a padded cell, barely ten feet on a side. There's a single bed, also white, which I was asleep in, but other than that the room is unfurnished. The walls, and even the door, are covered in squares of a white material that gleams like plastic, but which feels more like cloth when I reach out to touch it.

"What's happening, Jack?" I ask. "Do you know where we are?"

Jack shakes his head. "I woke up only a few minutes before you did." He moves around the room, checking it methodically. "There doesn't seem to be anything to give away where we are. I guess the best we can say is that if the people here wanted to kill us straight away, we'd already be dead."

That's matter of fact, but then, Jack has spent his life dealing with life and death situations. It's part of why he can stay so calm regardless of what's happening. Though I'd guess the part where he seems to be able to know what's about to happen a few seconds in advance helps there. It's easy not to be surprised by things when you know they're about to happen.

What surprises me is how calm I am then. I *don't* have Jack's years of working for the Underground, just a few short weeks of hiding out, trying to keep ahead of the Others who hunt down people like me. I'm seventeen, and I should be panicking, but I don't. I sit down calmly on the edge of the bed instead.

"I guess we'll just have to sit here and wait to see what happens then. Though I hope they hurry up. There isn't much time."

That doesn't even sound like me when I say it. It sounds like something an older version of me would say. No, I realize, it sounds like something the *dream* version of me, the one I saw before Jack woke me up, might say.

Even Jack seems to notice the difference because he looks at me oddly. Thoughtfully. "Celes," he says, "are you sure that you're okay?"

I nod. "I'm fine, I think. It's just… I was having a really strange dream before I woke up."

"Tell me?"

I shake my head. "It's nothing. Probably just whatever drug Lionel used."

"Probably," Jack says, sitting down beside me. That close, it's like I'm hyper-aware of his presence. I can hear every breath he takes. Normally, being that close to Jack is no problem for me. Normally, I'd let him slide an arm around me and comfort me. Here and now though, it's just a reminder of how little space there is. The calm I've been feeling now feels like its slipping away a bit at a time.

I stand up, moving around the room the way Jack did. I know he didn't find anything to show where we are, so there's no reason why I should, but right then, I can't sit still and wait any longer.

"Celes…"

I reach out for the door, with its panels of the strange white material. My fingers scrabble at the edge of one of them. If I can pull it away, maybe that will help.

"Celes, you need to calm down." Jack moves over to me and puts a hand on my shoulder. I feel that as the power in him calls to the power in me. My breath comes shorter and faster as it starts to feel like the walls are pressing in on me. I'm not normally claustrophobic, but I don't think I can deal with being in here much longer.

I can feel that burning power that sits in me then, pulsing up like the sap in a tree. In me, it feels so good, so natural, but I know what it can do.

"Jack," I manage, between those short, panting breaths, "get back. Get back *now*."

He steps back without asking why. Maybe he can feel what's coming.

The power leaps up in me, pouring out through my hand like water from a fire hose. Except that it isn't water that pours out of me. It's heat. Raw, impossible heat that I channel into the panels of the door with a white hot glow that would be blinding for almost anyone else. I can look into it easily though. I can look straight through it to see the damage I'm doing.

As usual, it feels so good to do this. So incredibly wonderful for something so utterly destructive. I can't help thinking back to the people I've used this power on.

Agents of the Others mostly. People who would have harmed or killed me if I hadn't. People I probably shouldn't feel too guilty about burning. At least this is only a door.

A very tough door, it turns out. The raw energy I carry inside me is enough to melt steel and disintegrate practically anything weaker, yet as it flares against the material of the door, I can see that it isn't so much as scorching it. That strange white material gets hot, so hot that I have to move my hand away, but it doesn't melt, or burn, or anything else. Whatever it is, it isn't like any material I've come across.

That makes me want to tear at it again and find out what it is. It feels like it's woven from fibers, but it's too dense and tough for most cloths. Trying to pull it away from the walls is still useless though. Worse than that, it's stupid. It just shows how panicked I am by now.

"Celes," Jack says. "It isn't working, Celes."

"If I can just..."

"It isn't working," Jack says again, and this time he puts his hands on my arms, pulling me away from the door. I want to pull away from him, and I want to press closer into his arms, all at the same time. In the end, I step back from him, standing in the corner of that tiny space, panting for breath. I normally feel so alive after using the power that I have, but right now, I just feel tired and scared. I'm trapped in a tiny room with no way to get out, and the whole space is just too small.

"It's going to be all right, Celes," Jack says.

"Is that a prediction?" I manage, and that gets a smile from him even though I probably shouldn't be talking about exactly what Jack can do right now. If this is a holding cell, then it's a pretty good bet that someone will be watching us. It occurs to me that not many eighteen year old girls would know that. I've obviously been spending too much time around secret organizations recently.

"It's just obvious." Jack's smile widens into an almost boyish grin. "After all, you're with me. What could possibly go wrong when you're with me?"

I start to list things on my fingers. "The first time we met face to face, an armored vehicle crashed through the wall, then you blew up your apartment. After that, I've been chased, shot at, my family has been attacked, and I've almost been killed a dozen times. So have you."

"True," Jack says, like none of it matters very much, "but almost doesn't really count, does it?"

I laugh at that, and as I start to calm down again, I realize that was probably what Jack was trying to achieve. That's the thing with Jack. He's wonderful. He's amazing to be around. He's handsome enough that sometimes I wonder why I'm the only one who was given a modeling career as a cover story by the Underground. Yet there's always that part of him that's thinking, that's calmly working out what needs to be done and doing it, no matter what else is going on. It means that whatever Jack does, it's hard not to look for that second motive behind it. Even when he's kissing me.

"So," I say, trying to match the lightness of his tone. If he can be strong here, I can be too, "I take it you've worked out a plan to get us both out of this cell by now?"

Jack shrugs. "I was thinking that we could always wait until they open the door."

"No, seriously," I say, starting to step forward to take another look at the material covering the door. Jack puts an arm out to stop me.

"Seriously," he says, looking at the door expectantly. I know that look, so I let him hold me back there for a second or two. A whirring sound comes from

- 18 -

the door, followed by a whoosh of air as some kind of seals disengage. I watch as it slides back like a screen door, disappearing into the wall beside it.

Jack gives another of those shrugs of his, and that perfect smile of his widens just a touch more. I have to admit, even when you're used to it, and even if it is just a second or two most of the time, seeing the future is pretty impressive.

THREE

The door opens, and someone starts to step through. They do so cautiously, as though they are expecting trouble, so that for the first second or two, all we can see is an arm covered by a suit sleeve, followed by a leg edging around the doorframe. No one who enters a room like that can intend anything good.

With all the speed of his Fader training and inherited power, Jack grabs the arm, dragging the newcomer into the room. It's a young man, with sandy blond hair and broad shoulders, but I don't have time to see more than that before Jack shoves him face first against the wall.

I dart for the open door, knowing that we might only get one chance at this. Even with the kind of speed that I have from the power within me, I'm not fast enough. The door slides shut with a hiss, so that my hands slam into the tiles of it once more. I can't even get a hand or foot in the way, though given the speed at which the door closes, maybe that's a good thing.

I cry out in frustration, almost at the same moment that Jack makes a noise of pain. I spin back to where he's pinning the man he grabbed, only to find that he isn't pinning him anymore. Almost as fast as Jack, the newcomer slams an elbow back into Jack's ribs, ducking under his arm to escape.

Jack fights back, and immediately things are chaos. The room just isn't big enough for a kind of elegant, calculated fight. Instead, everything has to be at close quarters, at a furious pace. Jack spins after the newcomer, grabbing him and driving him back to slam into the opposite wall, only for a knee to catch him in the stomach, making him double up. Jack drives upwards with the palm of his hand, but his opponent blocks the blow and comes back with a punch that Jack has to cover up to avoid.

That close, there's nothing pretty about fighting. Not that there ever is, but this is brutal. Jack and the newcomer shove against each other, heads down as they clinch, fists, elbows and knees flashing out with vicious speed as the two men struggle to land blows on each other. For the most part they aren't successful, as Jack and his opponent manage to parry, or just to grab the limb being used for the strike. There are so many blows being thrown though that more than a few get through, landing with meaty thuds and grunts of pain.

The man in the dark suit looks young and fit, so I doubt that will slow him down much. Jack either. I wince every time a punch hits him, half starting forward to try to help, but with so little space, I'm not sure I can help right then. Even that burning force inside me doesn't rise to the surface, as though recognizing that there isn't anything it can do. That's a scary thought, because it means that I've started thinking of the power inside of me as something that almost thinks for itself.

Briefly, Jack and his opponent break apart, but only so that they can go into a whirl of motion. Jack kicks low and then high, forcing the other man to cover his head and duck to avoid being hit. Jack jumps over a spinning sweep with ease, and then they crash back together, each struggling for the best grip on the other while simultaneously throwing punches and trying not to be hit in return.

The young man fighting Jack ducks down to try to tackle him around the legs. In that confined space though, there isn't the space to finish the move properly, and they both end up slumped against the base of the wall, still throwing punches. Jack's opponent rears up and I see my chance, pulling him back off Jack just long enough for Jack to gain the upper hand. Jack pounces forward, and they crash into the wall again, but this time Jack is on top.

Jack turns around, looking like he's offering his opponent an easy chance at a choke, but he's pressed back against his opponent so tightly that I can't even see the face of the young man he's fighting. Jack does something to entangle their legs, figure-fouring both of his around one of his opponent's before reaching down to grab the other with his hands. I have no idea what he's doing at that point.

Especially not when he executes a kind of forward roll down by his attacker's legs. One that sends both him and his opponent into a tangle of limbs, with Jack turning the other man above him like a juggler. The move ends with Jack clinging to his back, in position to start choking him. It also means that, for the first time since he came into the room, I get a clear view of the other man's face.

It's Grayson.

Grayson — my longtime former boyfriend, whom I had to leave behind when my family and I were faded, and I had to assume another identity...one of Celeste Channing, a socialite who was with Jack Simple, a Fader who was assigned to protect me. In a complicated twist of fate, Grayson came back into my life, and was faded into a highly-skilled Fader, like Jack.

I don't know what he's doing there, but it's him. I'd know the square jawed, rugged good looks beneath that sandy blond hair anywhere. His deep blue eyes look out at me and widen in surprise, even shock. They also widen in sudden fear at the strangle hold Jack is applying to him. I remember that they've been like that once before, out on the road when I was running with Grayson and he made the mistake of attacking Jack. Jack can be ruthless when he has to be. Weirdly, that's one of the things I love about him, because I know he is strong enough to survive in the world I've been plunged into.

Now though, it means that his arms are wrapped around Grayson's throat, squeezing.

"Jack!" I yell, knowing that in the rush of it all, I have to shout if I want Jack to listen. "Jack, it's Grayson. Let go."

Jack looks up at me blankly for a moment, then what I've just said seems to register, because he lets go, disentangling himself from Grayson slowly. Both of them scramble to their feet, looking worse for the fight. Jack has a cut above his left eye, which isn't large, but does drip blood until he presses a palm to it to stop the flow. Grayson has an ugly looking bruise on one cheek, and a graze along his jaw. Both of them wince slightly as they straighten up, and their clothes are a mess. Grayson's suit jacket is so badly torn that he takes it off and throws it aside, while Jack takes a moment or two to straighten his clothes.

"Grayson?" I rush forward to hug him, taking a moment to enjoy the clean, earthy scent of him so close. "What are you doing here? We went looking for you outside the farmhouse, but you weren't there. Then we were grabbed…"

"I swear that had nothing to do with me," Grayson says. He's looking at Jack as much as me when he says that. Maybe he just knows which of us is less likely to believe him. Though there were things he didn't tell me for years, too.

"Do you know where we are?" Jack asks. The way he says it is simple, professional. Just Jack. "You've been out in the corridors."

"I don't know too much," Grayson says. "I guess I only got here a little while before you did."

"What happened to you, Grayson?" I ask.

Grayson winces. "I was waiting for you on the farm when someone grabbed me from behind and put a bag over my head. I tried to fight. I knew..." he hesitates "... I knew I had to try to get back to the farmhouse to warn you."

"But you didn't," Jack points out. Is there a hint of accusation there?

"There were too many of them," Grayson says. "I got in a few punches, but then one of them must have knocked me out, because the next thing I knew I was waking up in a room."

"Describe it," Jack says.

Grayson shrugs. "Like this. Blank. White walled. A sliding door. I couldn't find any sign of where it was, if that's what you're asking."

"But you got out," I say, suddenly hopeful. If Grayson managed to get out of one cell, then maybe we can get out of this place too.

"Someone came in and I knocked him out," Grayson explains. He touches one of the bruises on his cheek. "You had the same plan, I guess."

I nod, but Jack's still asking questions.

"What happened when you got out of the holding cell? What did you see?"

"There were corridors," Grayson says. "I followed them around. I started trying doors, because I figured one of them had to lead out of here. Then you grabbed me."

"And now we're all trapped again," Jack says.

"I guess we'll just have to wait for the next escaping person to come along," I say, and laugh bitterly.

Jack reaches out to put a hand on my shoulder. "It's going to be fine, Celes."

"You hope."

"Have I ever let you down?" Jack looks back to Grayson, who doesn't look entirely happy about Jack comforting me, but who doesn't say anything. "What did you see out in the corridors? Can you help to pin down where we are?"

Grayson shakes his head. Watching the two of them there, I notice for the first time that Grayson seems to be deferring to Jack automatically, like a soldier with a superior officer. That has to be part of what the Faders did to him, implanting memories in him to train him to be one of them. Something tightens in me at that thought. It's kept Grayson alive, but what has it done to the real him? Is the boy who used to run with me still in there somewhere, or is he gone forever?

Of course, I'm not exactly the same girl I was then either. Between the physical changes the Faders made to me to disguise me and the power that comes out of me so easily now, I'm not the same Celestra Caine I was.

"So what did you see out there?" I ask.

"Nothing," Grayson says. "There's nothing out there. The corridors are coated in this... stuff..." he points to the panels on the doors "but there aren't any signs, or symbols, or anything like that. We could be anywhere."

"Not anywhere," Jack says with a shake of his head. "We know that this isn't one of the Underground's Locations, because I've never seen anywhere in one of those that looks like this. It doesn't *feel* like one of the Locations either."

From anyone else, that wouldn't have made much sense, but I've spent so long trusting Jack's feelings now that I don't even question it. What does that leave, though?

"The Others? But it was Lionel's people who took us, wasn't it?" A small knot of fear ties itself in my stomach at that thought. It can't be the Others, can it? The people who want me and Jack dead? The people Grayson's dad works for? It *can't* be them. If it is though, we need to get out of here right now.

As if in answer to that thought, Jack looks at the door. Grayson and I look too, because it's easy to guess what that means. Sure enough, the door slides open. And when it does so, my mouth falls open in sheer shock.

FOUR

I keep staring for several seconds, along with Grayson and Jack. I was expecting guards, or Lionel, or maybe even Grayson's father. I wasn't expecting *this*. I've never seen the man who stands in the doorway flanked by a couple of bodyguards face to face, but I know who he is. I guess right now, just about everybody on the planet knows who he is.

Wilson Hammond, former US senator, industrialist, and current presidential hopeful, is even more impressive in the flesh than he looks on the news. He's in his late fifties, though he looks fit and strong, and his dark hair doesn't show more than a few flecks of grey. His features are strong, with the kind of open, square jawed good looks that probably make life very easy for his campaign managers. His suit looks like it cost as much as most people's cars. He smiles as he steps into the room, but his deep blue eyes are watching us carefully. Those eyes of the two bodyguards with him definitely are. I can see the bulge of guns under their jackets. What does it say about my life that as an eighteen year old girl, I know to look for that?

"So, it's Celestra, Grayson and Jack, right?"

It takes me a moment to realize what he's just said. He's used my name. My real name. As far as the normal world is concerned, Celestra Caine never existed. She was erased when the Faders made me disappear. For everyone outside of the Others and the Underground, there's only Celeste Channing.

"You're probably wondering what you're doing here," Hammond continues.

"Actually," Jack says, "first I was wondering where 'here' was."

Hammond shakes his head. "Now, son, you know better than that, given what you do for a living."

"You know about Jack?" I ask, and the former senator turns a smile on me that he's probably practiced in a mirror. He holds out a hand, and one of the men with him hands him a file.

"I know about all of you, Celestra." He flicks through the file. "What the Others and the Underground do isn't common knowledge, but did you really think that no one in government keeps an eye on these things? There are committees, and sub-committees, and things less formal than that. I've been a part of some of them."

"So this is some kind of government run secret prison?" Grayson asks. Already, the bruises from his fight with Jack have faded, his body rebuilding itself the way it did back on the farm.

Hammond laughs. "You think that? No son, things aren't that bad. This is one of my company's facilities, and frankly I'm sorry that there's a need for this at all." He looks to each of us in turn. "Believe me, I didn't want to have you snatched and brought here, but there are times when a man has to make difficult decisions. Hopefully, you'll all be able to go home very soon."

Hopefully. It's kind of a frightening word, because it suggests that there are ways we might *not* be going home.

"What do you want from us?" I ask.

"From you, Celestra? Nothing. It's the fathers of these two young men whose help I need."

I don't quite get that, but Jack seems to. "You're interested in memory fading," he says.

"A good guess."

Jack shrugs. "It's what my father and Grayson's have in common."

"Because they worked together on the original experiments." Hammond turns over a page in the file he holds. "I know. When I first heard about it, I was skeptical, but I did my research. I found reports. Some of them were hard to get hold of, but I found them."

"So you want the details of fading," Jack says.

Hammond shakes his head. "I need someone faded."

"Who?"

He hesitates. Not for long, but he does. "My son."

Jack's expression doesn't change by much, but then, it never does. I reach out to put a hand on his arm before he does anything. He shakes his head. "No."

"You haven't heard why yet," Hammond points out.

"I've been through it," Jack says. He looks around at me and Grayson. "We all have, or at least they tried. Do you think we're going to put a kid through that?"

"I think your fathers already have," Hammond says. "So why not do it again? Fade my boy. Change his identity so well that even he doesn't know it."

I look at him, trying to make some sense of it. "Why? Why would you want to do that to your own son?"

Hammond nods. "That's a fair question. I guess it deserves an answer. You know I'm running for president? I have to ask, because kids sometimes don't pay as much attention to politics as they should."

"I know," I say. It's kind of hard not to, this close to the election. People seem to think that Wilson Hammond will win, too. They're already talking about what a great president he'll make. Right now, pretty obviously, I'm not so sure.

"Well, I've worked very hard to keep Johnny out of the public eye so far," Hammond explains, "but that isn't going to be enough if I win the presidency. I'll do whatever I have to do in order to shield him from that kind of scrutiny. He doesn't deserve to grow up like that."

"So you want to fade him?" Jack says. "You want to send him away and take away every memory of you?"

Hammond looks angry for a moment. "Of course I don't *want* to, but it's necessary. You sound just like your father."

"You've already spoken to Sebastian about this?" I ask.

"And he said no?" I ask.

"He said no," Hammond agrees. "And Grayson's father Richard did not have the fading machine. Which is where the three of you come in."

"As hostages."

Hammond shrugs. "That's an ugly word, but I guess it's an ugly situation. So this is what's going to happen. You, Jack, obviously know more about all this than the other two, and I think your father is the better bet anyway, so I'm going to let you go."

"So that I can help fade a little boy?" Jack demands. He shakes his head. "That isn't going to happen, Hammond. What you're suggesting... it's wrong."

"It's what's right for my son."

Another shake of the head from Jack. "It's what's right for you, but trust me, I've been there, and there is no way that this is what is best for the boy."

"*I* decide what's best for my son," Hammond snaps. He gestures to the two men with him and they hurry forward. One of them heads straight at me. I go to punch him but he manages to block the blow, driving into me and pinning me back against the wall through sheer bulk. He spins me around, wrenching one of my arms behind my back.

I want to burn him then. I want it, but I force myself to squash the feeling. I'm not killing anyone. Not here. Even if what Wilson Hammond is doing is wrong, I'm not killing him and his men just for trying to help his son. That doesn't mean I won't fight though. I stamp down with my foot on the shin of the man grabbing me, then try to drive my elbow back into him.

He holds tightly, and I feel something cold and metallic snap around my left wrist. He grabs my right, and too late I realize what he's doing. He's handcuffing me. For a moment, I start to panic, but then I realize that it isn't a problem. I even stop fighting, letting him put the cuff on my other wrist and waiting until he lets go of me. I turn around, to see that Grayson is cuffed too, while Wilson Hammond is watching the whole thing impassively.

Then I burn.

I call up the power inside me, call to it until I can feel it blazing out through my eyes. Call to it and stare straight at Wilson Hammond so that he can see what he is dealing with, while I send that power into the handcuffs holding me. I figure that a pool of molten metal on the floor ought to persuade him that he shouldn't be threatening us. So I drive the power in me down into that metal, waiting for it to fall from my wrists in ruins.

I keep going like that for almost a minute before I remember what happened with the walls. Before I realize that the cuffs aren't even getting very hot, let alone melting away from my skin.

"What..." I begin, but by then it's obvious that what I'm doing is useless, so I call the power back into me. No, not call. Drag. It's an effort to shove it back down inside me when it hasn't destroyed anything. An effort that leaves beads of sweat standing out on my forehead.

Hammond stares at me, not in shock, but with obvious satisfaction. "One of the research companies I own has been doing work with advanced materials. Once it became clear that we might need to snatch you, Celestra, it seemed like those would come in useful."

Meaning that I'm trapped. Again, just the thought of that is enough to make fear spring up in me, enough that my breath comes quickly, and it's hard to even think.

"Try to relax," Hammond says, stepping past Jack as he starts to move to comfort me. "You aren't in any danger right now, young lady."

"It's all right," Jack says, finally reaching me. "It's going to be fine, Celes." He looks over at Hammond. "This is totally unnecessary."

Hammond shakes his head. "I disagree. For one thing, I hope it shows you how serious I am about this. For another, it means that Celestra and Grayson here won't be knocking out any more of my men. It also means that they're able to come out of the cell when we need them to in order to allow us to study what Celestra can do."

"Study me?" I take a step back towards the wall automatically. "I'm not a guinea pig."

"But what you can do is fascinating," Hammond says. "I'd like to be able to better understand it. If you're really generating power from nowhere, it could potentially benefit a lot of people."

"Leave Celes alone." Jack and Grayson say that almost simultaneously. Grayson starts forward, but is dragged back by the minder who has cuffed him. Jack moves closer to Hammond.

"You want to think very carefully about what you're doing," Jack says. "If you know who the Underground are, and you know who the Others are, then you'll know that you don't want either group for enemies.

Let Celes and Grayson go, and I'll see what I can do for your son."

Hammond shakes his head. "You've already shown that you aren't interested in doing that, so we have to do things the other way. Bring me the means to alter my son's memories, get your father to agree to help, or these two stay locked up. Help me, and they can go. I'm not interested in hurting them. If you're in a mood to make threats though, remember this. Soon I'll be the president of the United States, with all the resources that go with that. Trust me, son, you don't want to go there."

Jack stands there for several seconds. Is he calculating how to break us all out of there? Is he planning a sudden attack? No, it seems he isn't. He nods instead.

"I'll do what you ask."

FIVE

Hammond steps aside, gesturing to the door. "It's time for you to go, Jack."

Jack nods. "In a second."

He steps over to me, putting his arms around my neck and staring into my eyes. Somehow, it always comes as a surprise to see how much he loves me in moments like that. Maybe it's just that he keeps his emotions so shut down the rest of the time, or maybe it's just that I can't get the hang of anyone loving me that deeply. He leans in and kisses me sweetly, simply. Then, just for a moment or two, his lips brush my ear.

"Don't trust Hammond," he whispers. "His story might have some truth in it, but there's more going on here. I'm sure of it."

I can't answer. All I can do is hold onto Jack a moment longer.

"That's enough," Hammond says. "Assuming Jack here does as I've asked, then you'll see one another again soon enough."

Jack pulls away and steps through the door to the cell ahead of Hammond. The two bodyguards follow. The instant they're through that gap, the door slides shut again, trapping me and Grayson in that tiny, empty cell. Only now we're both cuffed as well, which is anything but comfortable. I can't help testing the limits of the things, so that pretty soon, my wrists start to chafe from being held like that. I sit down on the edge of the bed, trying to force myself to relax. It doesn't work. I can't relax in a place like this, not with what's going on around us.

"Jack will be back," Grayson says, obviously seeing how worked up I'm getting.

That makes me smile. "I never thought I'd see the day when you'd rely on Jack."

Grayson manages to shrug, even handcuffed. "He cares about you, Celes. I'm not going to deny that. He'll do whatever it takes to get you to safety. Just remember that I would too."

That's hard to forget, though thanks to being faded, Grayson managed it for a while. Now though, he obviously remembers everything, which doesn't make things any easier, because I love Jack. I *love* him, more than just about anything. I can remember what I had with Grayson, and the way it ended... well, that wasn't good, but it's Jack my heart beats faster at the thought of, even though he isn't here.

"Do you think they're just going to leave us like this?" I ask.

Grayson shakes his head. "They can't. Not for long, anyway. I'm more worried about what Hammond said about running tests on you."

"Maybe he just said that to frighten Jack."

"Maybe." Grayson doesn't look convinced. "I can't believe this guy's running for president and he's still willing to do this."

"Whatever he's doing, it must be a big deal," I say.

Grayson nods. "Jack doesn't think he's telling the truth, does he?"

I shake my head. "You heard him?"

"I heard him."

"What I don't get," I say, "is how Hammond knows so much about us. He knows about the Faders and the Others. Do you think what he said about there being secret committees that know about them is true?"

"Probably," Grayson says, like it makes sense. I guess it does, kind of. I can't believe that two organizations as big as the Others and the Underground could exist without someone knowing about them, and the government would want to keep a watch on any group that large and powerful, even if it never did anything about it.

"Of course," Grayson says, "it could be something else."

"Like what?"

"He could be connected to the Underground or the Others directly."

I hadn't thought of it that way, but it makes a kind of sense. Hammond could be lying. It could all be a set-up of some kind. But if so, what is he trying to achieve. All he's done so far is get Jack to go fetch his father. But isn't that enough?

"It could be the Others," I say.

Grayson looks at me questioningly. "Why them? Why not the Underground?"

I try to explain, but I'm not sure it makes that much sense. "Because he only let Jack out. Why not send both of you? Your dad might not be Sebastian Cook, but he might still be able to help with fading someone. If he let you both go and kept me, wouldn't that improve his odds of one of you coming back with the kind of help he says he wants?"

"Maybe he thinks he needs more hostages," Grayson suggests.

"Or maybe it's Sebastian that he wants," I say.

Grayson finally seems to get it, a look of surprise crossing his square jawed features. "You mean that this could all be about trying to capture Jack's father again?"

"Why not?" I say. "If the Others sent some kind of team to the farm to snatch him, but they couldn't find him, maybe taking us was the next best thing."

"Or maybe it isn't the Others at all," Grayson points out.

I shut my eyes for a moment. "Maybe not. I guess I just want this to be simple. It's easier if I can blame it on the Others, I guess."

Grayson smiles at me like he understands. "I know. If it's all the Others, rather than some guy just deciding to do this, then it's easy. We beat them and it's over. If it isn't just them, then where does it end?"

That's it exactly. If I can blame this, and everything else, on just one twisted organization, then life gets easier. It means that things can be solved easily. It means that I don't have to accept that normal people can do bad things. Like Grayson said, Hammond is meant to be running for president. If a man doing that can do something like this, then what about everyone else? No, I can't think like that, or I'll go crazy.

"You know what I think?" Grayson says, standing up.

I shake my head. "What?"

"I think we need to start work on getting out of here again. That way, no matter what's going on, we aren't in the middle of it. We can warn Jack and his father."

He's right. Of course he's right. But saying it and doing it are two different things. It seems like we don't have time, either, because in that moment the door to the cell opens again to let in one of the large men who came in with Wilson Hammond. His blond hair is buzz-cut short, his muscles bulge through his suit, and he's wearing wraparound shades as well as black gloves that don't really fit with the suit. Grayson half turns towards him... and then collapses to the floor unconscious as the bodyguard punches him right on the jaw.

"Hey, what are you doing?" I demand, but in that moment he takes a swing at me too. I barely dodge it, feeling the rush of air as the punch goes past my head. I get a good look as it happens of Grayson there on the floor, completely out. I know he's going to be fine. I know he'll heal, but right then, that sight is enough to send fury bursting through me.

Something in me snaps and I charge at the bodyguard. My hands are still tied behind me, and he's far bigger than I am, far stronger. Right then that doesn't matter. I slam my shoulder into him, and the power in me is already rushing through me hard enough that I knock him back into the opposite wall, shoving into him. He spins me around, pulling me back tight against him with gloved hands, but that doesn't matter. If anything, it makes things easier.

I lift my cuffed hands behind me, placing them on the shirt of the man attacking me. Grabbing hold of it so he won't get away. I don't want him to just stop after what he's done. I want him dead. It's so easy to use my power in that moment. As easy as it has been when Jack has been in danger before. So easy that it would be harder *not* to use it. I take that force, and it pours out of my hands into the man holding me. Before, I didn't want to do this, but now, when he's hurt Grayson like that... now nothing can stop me.

The man cries out in pain as a white hot glow surrounds us both. He cries out, but he holds on, keeping a tight grip on me while his arm wraps around my throat. He makes a sound that is more animal than human, so full of pain that it's amazing he can still stand, but he manages to start squeezing anyway.

I can't breathe. I can't breathe, and he's still squeezing, even though I'm pouring all the energy I can out of my hands. He'll stop soon though. He'll stop when there's nothing left of him but ashes. The part of me that thinks that seems far too happy about it, but right then, the rest of me is busy working hard not to pass out. If I can just hold on a little longer...

He isn't burning. Why isn't he burning? There's heat there, because he's obviously in pain, but he isn't disintegrating. He isn't dying. He's even able to keep squeezing so that I fight and struggle, straining for breath. It feels like there's far too much pressure in my head. Like I'm going to explode. I can see hints of blackness on the edges of my vision, and it's hard to concentrate on just keeping the power going. So hard. Even harder than fighting for oxygen.

My mind starts to drift, and I realize something feels strange about the cloth of the bodyguard's suit where his elbow it tucked under my chin. For a fraction of a second it seems like nothing more than the random observation of a brain quickly shutting down, but then I remember what Wilson Hammond said about his company working on new materials. The suit must be made from the same stuff as the walls, meaning...

Meaning that even if I'm hurting the man attacking me, it isn't going to stop him. He's protected by his suit. He won't burn, no matter how much energy I use in doing it. I need to... need to...

It's too late. I gasp for air, but it's too late. I was so certain that I could break free. So certain, and so angry. Now, I can't think. Can't even move. My legs give way, and for the next few seconds the bodyguard holds me up so that he can keep squeezing. Then he lowers me to the ground beside Grayson. I stare up at him and he frowns down at me.

"Still awake?" he says. His face looks red, like he's been sunburnt, but he doesn't sound like he's in pain right then. "Well, I guess we can deal with that."

He leans over me and I will my body to respond, but right then it simply doesn't seem to be able to. He draws one gloved hand back carefully, then I feel the punch slam into my jaw, the way it connected with

Grayson's earlier. This time the darkness washes over me completely, and I don't feel anything after that.

SIX

When I open my eyes, Grayson is there, staring down at me with obvious concern. His hands are on my shoulders. My jaw aches, and I groan as he helps me to sit up. I look around. We're sitting on a flat orange couch at one side of a large room with brightly colored walls made of the same material as the cell, a breakfast bar at one end, an open door that appears to lead through to some kind of bathroom, and in between...

In between, it's like the kind of room a teenager might come up with if they were given an unlimited budget to play with. There's a huge TV dominating one wall, with a rack of games consoles under it that looks like it could run a spaceship. There's an armchair so big that it looks almost like a joke, and a low pool table off in one corner. There are boxes around the walls, which look like they could contain almost anything. The whole place looks like it was designed to entertain someone who was very, very rich.

Is this designed to make us comfortable? It looks like a great kind of place, but I notice that my hands are still cuffed. They've been moved in front of me, giving me a small amount of movement, but the cuffs are rigid metal ones, which make it hard to do much with my hands. So this isn't just about our comfort. Or maybe it is, but there are definitely limits to it. The heat resistant material on the walls and the lack of an obvious exit both make that very clear.

"You're awake," Grayson says. "I was starting to worry. I had to plead with them before they'd even let me put an ice pack on your bruising."

"Do you know where we are?" I ask, before my mind moves to the obvious question. "Why am I still cuffed?"

"Sorry," Grayson says, helping me to stand. "I tried to get them to un-cuff you, but they said you were too dangerous. I think they're scared of what you can do, Celes. My ability doesn't seem to frighten them as much."

"They know about what you can do?" I ask, and Grayson gestures to his face, then very gently touches my jaw. I wince.

"It was kind of obvious, I guess," Grayson says. I guess that it would have been, with the bruises on him fading completely while mine blossomed. I can kind of understand Wilson Hammond's men not seeing it as threatening, either. After all, the ability to heal injuries might be useful, but it isn't exactly a weapon. Whereas if I could touch exposed skin...

Well, I'd probably still be trapped in whatever room I was in. The materials from Hammond's companies are almost perfect, when it comes to stopping me. I just wish that they hadn't managed to come up with handcuffs made from the stuff.

"I guess that they've been observing us for a little while too," Grayson says. "They probably saw what happened back at the farmhouse."

The farmhouse. Where I used my power on Grayson by accident. Where he survived it along with everything that one of Lionel's rogue Faders could throw at him. Where Jonah told me that my powers might not be alien after all, but merely something thousands of years beyond anything humanity had evolved into so far. Did I tell Grayson that part? I start as I realize that I didn't. He deserves to know.

"Grayson…"

I don't finish that thought, because at that point a door opens in a section of wall where I hadn't even spotted a door when I was looking around. A woman steps through. She has short blonde hair and is probably in her mid-thirties, wearing a relatively simple dark dress and looking at us both slightly nervously. She's carrying a tray, on which there are two plates containing what looks like meatloaf.

"Hi," I say, and she starts slightly. I'm not sure why she would, except that of course I'm wearing handcuffs, and she's probably been told just how dangerous I am. Maybe she's even been told outright not to talk to us. She certainly hurries out of the room once she's put the plates down on the breakfast counter.

It occurs to me then that we could have escaped in that moment. Trained bodyguards might be too much for me and Grayson, but one maid, or cook, or assistant wouldn't be. But I'm not going to do that. Hurting her won't solve anything. There are probably people waiting outside the door just in case we try it, and in any case, she obviously isn't one of Hammond's thugs. It wouldn't be right.

I'm starving, and I head over to the counter, trying to work on the meatloaf as best I can with my hands still cuffed. It's awkward. Really awkward. So awkward in fact that in the end Grayson spears a bit of it with his fork and offers it to me.

"Here," he says, "let me help."

I eat it gratefully, and the bite after that. It's such an intimate thing, sitting there with Grayson feeding me like that. It reminds me of when we were back at school together, in the cafeteria, and I would steal bits of food off his plate. Or of the kind of romantic meal you see in movies. Except that there, the woman generally isn't handcuffed.

We eat, and after a while the door opens again, letting the woman in with what looks like dessert. Large slices of chocolate cake topped with cherries. It isn't exactly prison food. She puts it down without a word and leaves, but I don't get the chance to eat the forkful of the stuff Grayson picks up, because at that moment we have more visitors. Senator Hammond is there, along with his two thugs.

I stand up, ready for whatever confrontation he has in mind, when a much smaller figure steps past the

Senator. It's a small boy, probably no more than seven or eight years old, with messy brown hair, blue eyes that make it clear whose son he is, and a broad smile. He's wearing a blue t-shirt, jeans and sneakers.

The boy moves over to the games consoles and they spring into life. He looks at his father, and Senator Hammond nods indulgently.

"My son, Johnny," he says, by way of an explanation. "He never does seem to be able to resist a round of Battlewar."

"It's hard to blame him," Grayson says. "It's a good game. Hey, Johnny, I'm Grayson. Can I join in?"

I can't help smiling at that as Grayson settles down next to the giant armchair, playing the game along with the senator's son. He's good with the kid, but then, he's always managed to get along with just about everyone. That's what made Grayson him, the track star, and my former long-term boyfriend. Senator Hammond and I are left watching while the two of them blow up imaginary alien enemies for a while. Eventually though, the senator puts a hand on his son's shoulder.

"I think that's enough for now, Johnny. It's time for you to meet Celestra."

"Celes," he says. "She prefers Celes."

I do, but I'm not sure how he knows that.

"She's the one, isn't she dad?"

Senator Hammond shakes his head. "It's best if you don't know that, Johnny."

"Why?"

"It's hard to explain."

"But she's special, right?" Johnny asks. "She's special like me?"

I look at Senator Hammond sharply. What does his son mean by that?

"I guess you would know better than anyone, Johnny," the senator says. His son looks up at me with those big, blue, excited eyes and for the first time since I've gotten here, it doesn't feel like everyone is afraid of me. Johnny just looks fascinated.

He frowns slightly. "Why is she handcuffed like that, Dad? Did she do something wrong?"

Senator Hammond ruffles his son's hair. "It's not like that, Johnny. That's to protect us. Celes here is potentially very dangerous, and I have to make sure that she doesn't hurt anyone."

"I don't think she'd hurt me," Johnny ventures. "I don't think she likes being locked up. I wouldn't."

Senator Hammond looks at me long and hard. "I don't think she would hurt you either, but she might hurt other people. Maybe without even meaning to. And we don't always get to do things we like. Sometimes we have to do things we don't like, because that's what's best."

Johnny nods, but I wonder if he really understands it. He's just a kid, after all. A kid whose father is talking about wiping away his memories. Why would he do that? Why would any father do that to his son? I guess for an answer to that, I'd have to ask Sebastian Cook. It's what he did to Jack, after all.

"Does doing things you don't want to include having your men beat us unconscious?" Grayson asks, standing up and moving to join us.

Senator Hammond looks at him sharply. I can guess why. He isn't going to want his son to hear what he had done. Most fathers want to be heroes to their sons for as long as possible. It's hard to stay a hero when you're having people hurt.

"My men were... overzealous," he says. "It seemed like the most efficient, and least risky, way of moving you.

You have my word that it will not happen in quite that way again."

His word. I guess we're all relying on his ability to keep his word. He's said he'll let me and Grayson go when Jack gets back. He's said we won't be hurt. It would be so easy for him to lie, but right now, we just don't have any choice other than to trust him. There's one thing I have to know, though.

"You didn't answer Johnny before," I say. "Am I special like him? Are we both special the same way?"

"Is she, Dad?" Johnny demands, pulling on his father's arm. "Is she special like I'm special?"

Senator Hammond doesn't look pleased by that either, but he nods. "Almost, Johnny. She isn't quite the same as you are, and nor is her friend, but they're both special in their own ways."

"Then why am *I* the one who has to forget?" Johnny asks. Either his father has told him what is going to happen to him, or he has overheard it the way kids hear so much. "If I'm so special, why do I have to *stop* being special?"

"Trust me, Johnny," his father says, "it will be easier this way. Your gift is very powerful, but it will hurt you. You'll live every day knowing things that will only cause you pain. It's better if you forget all about it."

"But I don't want to forget," Johnny says. "I don't want to stop being me."

"I don't want that either," Senator Hammond says, "but I said it before. Sometimes we have to do things that we don't really want to, because they're the best things." He looks up at me and Grayson in turn. "I brought Johnny here so that you would understand what this means to me. You won't be here for long. Come on, Johnny."

With that, he leads his son from the room, taking his guards with him and leaving me and Grayson alone there. I watch them go, and I can barely stop myself from saying something. What he's planning… it's wrong. It was wrong when Sebastian did it to Jack. It was wrong when Richard did it to Grayson, and it's no less wrong now. The trouble is, I don't think that there's anything we can do about it.

SEVEN

Maybe ten minutes after Senator Hammond leaves, his men come back into the room. One of them is holding a pair of blindfolds.

"What are those for?" Grayson asks.

"We're moving you to your quarters for tonight," the bodyguard says. "Would you prefer it if we did it the same way as before?"

The threat is obvious, so Grayson and I both stand there while they blindfold us. One of the men takes me by the arm, leading me along a complicated route I can't keep track of. I guess that we're going back to our cell. Except that, when we stop and one of the men pulls my blindfold off, that's not where we are.

This room is almost on the scale of the one we've just come from, and a couple of doors in the far wall suggest that there is more space beyond. The whole place is furnished like an apartment, from the big white couch and TV to the small kitchen space at the back of the room.

It actually reminds me a little of the place I briefly shared with Jack when I was pretending to be Celeste Channing, except that apartment had a view, while this one is windowless so that we can't tell where we are.

"The senator says that if you don't cause trouble, you're to be treated as guests," one of the bodyguards says.

"Does that mean I get un-cuffed?" I ask.

He answers that with a quick shake of his head, and the two of them leave. The door shuts firmly behind them.

"Guests don't get locked in," Grayson says, moving around the place, looking it over.

"But I guess prisoners don't normally get places as nice as this," I point out. I shake my head. "They must be pretty scared of me if they're making me leave the cuffs on here. It's going to make things tricky."

Grayson moves close to me. "I'll help you as much as you need. You know that."

I do, but it's going to be strange relying on someone, even Grayson, that completely. Of course, when I was living with Jack, I relied on him in a different way, with my safety completely in his hands. I guess it still kind of is.

In the next few hours, I'm grateful Grayson is there. With my hands still cuffed, even the most basic things become almost impossible. He has to feed me again, and I can barely manage to change the channel on the TV without him. Without him, I would be almost helpless.

Yet I'm not sure that's enough of a reason for him to be there. I still don't get why Senator Hammond didn't send him out to get help from his father. That or just let him go completely, because that would surely have sent a good message. It would have told Jack and his father that he was serious about letting us go when he could.

I eventually ask Grayson that question outright. "Why do you think the senator is keeping you here?"

Grayson shakes his head. "I don't know. It's not like he can think it makes it more likely Jack will come back. Jack's going to come back anyway for you. He doesn't even like me that much. I guess it could be a tactical thing, so that I don't try to lead any kind of rescue, but even that doesn't make much sense, because having me here makes it more likely that the Others will try something. If he let me go, I'd just have the Faders helping, the same as Jack."

It's hard getting used to this version of Grayson; one who can talk about tactical ideas as well as any Fader.

It's him, but it's not him somehow. It's not the boy I grew up with, and I find myself wondering if we'll ever get that boy back. If Grayson will ever go back to having a normal life; maybe go off to college. It's weird. I think that about Grayson, but I don't think it about myself. Maybe it's because whatever is happening to me is a part of me. I can't get away from that, even if I want to.

The hardest part about those hours there with Grayson isn't the cuffs on my wrists. It isn't the way he has to help me so much. It's being so close to him in a situation like this. Even though we've been forced into it, even though there's nothing we can do to change it, we're effectively sharing an apartment together. And I already know how well that can push people together. Just look at me and Jack.

If I hadn't met Jack, and none of this had happened, would we have ended up like this one day? Not captured by some senator with an agenda of his own, but in an apartment somewhere? Would we have shared a place when we went to college? We were planning on it, but that seems like years ago now, even though it has just been a month or two.

We sit together on the sofa, not quite pressed together, but not quite apart, either. The news is on the TV. There's so much pain on there. There's news from half a dozen warzones around the world, a couple of disaster relief efforts in places that have been struck by earthquakes or floods, as well as news on a famine caused by drought in Africa.

"It kind of makes you appreciate what you have," Grayson says, flipping the channels.

I nod. "I guess so. I mean, we live in a wealthy country, which hasn't been affected too badly by things like climate change. When you look at all the other people in the world suffering, I guess we aren't doing too badly."

"Except for the handcuffs," Grayson points out.

"Except for that." I shrug. "I guess even there... well, we're in a nice apartment, and we don't know that anyone's planning on killing us. There are a lot of places people would do worse things."

Grayson keeps channel hopping, and something catches my eye.

"Grayson, wait."

He stops, and we watch as a news piece starts to go on about Senator Hammond's efforts in disaster zones.

It's spliced together footage of him in Ethiopia, in Japan... in just about every spot in the world where people are suffering. There are speeches from him promising not just that he will talk to the Senate about getting help for them, but actively promising chunks of his own vast fortune to help.

"It would be kind of impressive if he didn't have us locked up," I say.

Grayson nods. "You know they say he's certain to win the presidency now? I'm not sure what to think about that. I mean, he does all this in the world..."

"But he still has us locked up." I nod. "I know. It was easier with the Others. At least they were just there to try to kill us. Me, anyway. The worst part..."

"Go on," Grayson says.

"The worst part is, what if he's right, locking me up like this? I burn people, Grayson. I burn them to ashes. What if he's right to take all these precautions? What if they're all right, and I'm nothing but dangerous? Half the time, it doesn't even feel like I'm in control of what I do."

There's so much that has happened in the past few weeks. So much that has changed. It hits me in a rush. I'm determined that I'm not going to cry, but it's hard not to when we're stuck there like that. Especially when Grayson, seeming to sense my mood, puts an arm around me to comfort me. I still don't cry there, but there isn't much difference. I hold onto him and I just try to forget the world for a while. It's always like this around Grayson. He's always had the knack of making me feel safe, and calm, and...

I look up and he's so close. Close enough that it just seems natural to move that little bit closer. To kiss him. He kisses me back, our lips meeting and moving, while his hands stroke through my hair. He pulls back for half a second, then kisses me again, harder this time, and we fall so that we're lying down on the couch now, with him above me.

"Gray, no. Wait."

I pull back from him, moving out from under him and standing up.

"What is it?" he asks.

I shake my head. "I can't. I just can't. I'm with Jack. I mean, we haven't really confirmed anything, but..."

"If it isn't official, then you can do what you want," Grayson says, moving to kiss me again. I dodge him. He doesn't look happy about that. "Don't try to tell me that you don't feel anything for me after all we've been through, Celes."

I don't answer immediately. Instead I step away. "Look, this isn't the right time, or the right place. I need to go wash up, and then I think I'm going to go get some sleep. Please don't make this awkward, Gray."

I hurry off, finding the bathroom. I won't be able to undress properly when I'm still cuffed, so a full shower or bath is out. That means doing the best I can with a washcloth. Except that, after a minute or two, it becomes painfully obvious that I'm not going to be able to wash myself like that, because I simply can't use my hands well enough. That means that I either forget about cleaning myself up completely, or I ask Grayson for help. So soon after what has just happened, that feels so awkward that I actually have another try at washing up on my own. It doesn't work any better than the first try did.

"Gray?"

He hurries in, and his eyes linger on me for just a moment, but he manages to recover well when he sees my predicament. "Here," he says, "let me help."

He takes the washcloth from me and manages a kind of sponge bath with it. "I'm sorry about before," he says. "I know that it's a really awkward position for you, and I know you have a lot going on. Even if you don't feel the same way about me as I do about you, then I still want to be your friend."

Well, *that* doesn't make things any more comfortable. In fact, the whole thing is one of the most awkward few minutes of my life so far. I'm so close to Grayson, but I'm about as far from him in that moment as I've ever been, even though we're physically touching.

I guess the sensible thing to do then would be to stay away from him once we're done, but I can't even do that. I go to sit with him on the sofa after a while, and we watch TV together again. That *is* a bit like being with the old Grayson, because we'd sit together on each other's couches forever, just being close to one another. I don't even notice the moment when I fall asleep.

I wake with Grayson shaking me.

"Celes, wake up."

"What? What is it?"

"You don't remember? You were screaming. You were yelling for people to take shelter."

I start to say that I don't remember, but I do. The dream comes back to me as he says it. Something was coming, and I was the older me that I've seen so many times in my dreams before. The man whose face I can never see was there too, except that now, now it seems so obvious. I look at Grayson.

"You were there. You were there with me all the time."

EIGHT

I get the bed in the room's adjoining bedroom for the night, while Grayson takes the couch. Not that I sleep that well with my hands still cuffed. In the morning, Senator Hammond's men come to fetch us, blindfolding us again so that they can take us back to the entertainment room they left us in yesterday. Breakfast is waiting for us, in the form of fruit and pastries, coffee and juice, all laid out on the counter at the side of the room. We eat, and before long, the door open, letting in the senator. His bodyguards stand back in the corners of the room, watching.

"I'm not going to ask if you slept okay," he says. "That would be hypocritical of me. I hope your night here wasn't too bad, though."

"So long as you get what you want, do you even care?" Grayson asks.

One of Senator Hammond's bodyguards starts forward, but the senator raises a hand to stop him. "I'm not going to lie to you. I need access to the device used to fade memories. I will do whatever I need to do to achieve that, but I won't hurt either one of you unnecessarily."

That isn't exactly comforting. Especially not when he's already kept us here as prisoners for the night, and his men have beaten us both unconscious once. I have to ask the obvious question though. "Is there any news of Jack? Has he gotten back to the Faders yet?"

Senator Hammond looks a little uncomfortable in that moment. "Ah. That's the thing, Celestra. We dropped Jack back near the Location where we took the three of you an hour or two after he left here. I should have heard something from him by now. At least if he's taking me seriously."

"What are you saying?" Grayson asks.

"I'm saying that I think your friend is playing games with me," Senator Hammond says, "and I don't have time for that. None of us do. So I'm going to have to find a way to persuade him to hurry things up a little."

I don't like the sound of that. Especially not when one of the bodyguards steps forward, reaching into his jacket. I've seen movies before, so I can guess at the kind of things a kidnapper might do to hurry Jack up. My stomach clenched and I can feel my body stiffen, getting ready act if necessary. So much for saying he didn't plan to hurt us.

Except that the bodyguard doesn't come out with some kind of weapon. Instead, he passes the senator a flat touch screen.

"What's that for?" I ask.

Senator Hammond turns it so that I can see it. "Watch and you'll understand."

Images start across the screen, obviously taken from security cameras in the space they gave us to sleep in. There's a section of me curled up on the couch with Grayson watching TV, looking like we're a happy couple having a cozy night in together. Another part captures us kissing.

"Why are you doing this?" I demand. "That isn't how it happened."

Senator Hammond shrugs. "There's more."

The next section is from the bathroom. I almost know what's coming before it starts. Grayson helping me. Grayson washing me when I can't do it myself thanks to the cuffs. It looks… it looks like the kind of thing that would really hurt Jack. My face burns red just at the thought of it, with both embarrassment and anger. Embarrassment that someone was watching all through that. Anger that Hammond is planning to use it against us.

"You can't send that," I say. "Please don't send it."

Senator Hammond shakes his head. "I told you. I'll do whatever I have to do."

"But Celes didn't *do* anything!" Grayson complains.

"She kissed you."

"*I* kissed *her*." Grayson shakes his head. "I made all the moves yesterday. Celes didn't want anything to do with it. She's with Jack."

"Which is why he'll come running," Senator Hammond points out. He tosses the reader to Grayson, who catches it but doesn't destroy it. "Ah, clever boy. The original is already on its way, of course."

"But you can't do this," I say. "I mean, you're running for *president*."

For a second, just a second, Senator Hammond looks a little ashamed, but it doesn't last. "How do you think people get to high office, Celestra? You think that any one of my political rivals would hesitate if they got hold of footage showing me doing something compromising?"

"But I'm not running for office. You just grabbed me and..."

"And with everything that's at stake, you should be grateful I'm going for an option that doesn't hurt anything other than your relationship," Senator Hammond snaps. "All we do is send Jack this and he'll hurry back. He won't want to risk the possibility that there could really be romance in the air."

I look at him, and for a moment or two, I hate him. Hate him for what he's done, and for what that might mean for me and Jack. I'm curious too, though. "How can you know Jack that well?"

Senator Hammond hands back the screen to his bodyguard. "We watched you before we took you, and I'm good at judging people. I saw the way Jack looked at you."

"You watched us?"

He sighs, shaking his head. "I said before, the Others and the Faders aren't the only ones with an interest here. Frankly, I doubt either of them really knows how dangerous you are. How dangerous you could be, anyway."

"And you do?" Grayson says, moving so that he's between me and the senator.

Hammond nods. "The part they don't understand is that what makes you dangerous isn't your ability to burn people, or your speed. It's far more than that."

I gently move Grayson out of the way. I'm not going to let someone like the senator intimidate me. "You sound like you know a lot about me."

"More than you could possibly know." The senator's expression softens a little. "But then, I had a better source of information than anyone else."

I've only seen his expression go that way around one thing so far here. "This has something to do with Johnny," I guess.

Senator Hammond looks a little surprised, but then nods. He makes a sign to one of his bodyguards, and the man goes to the door. It opens and Johnny runs in. He looks so excited to be there, though from the way he's looking at the games console I guess he's mostly just looking forward to another game of Battlewar with Grayson. Especially with the pleading look he gives his dad.

"Not right now, Johnny." Senator Hammond looks at me. "Promise me that you'll behave yourself, Celestra. Promise me."

What? Does he really think that I'm going to do something to hurt a little kid?

"I'm not the one trying to wipe his memory," I say, but one look at Senator Hammond's expression tells me that he's serious. "Okay, I promise."

The senator looks around at his two bodyguards. "Out, both of you."

"Senator..."

"Out. I understand the risks, and right now I'm willing to take them. What I'm not willing to risk is someone overhearing this conversation who doesn't need to be here. So make sure that we aren't disturbed for any reason. Understood?"

The bodyguard doesn't look happy about it. I guess that he's worried I'll try to attack his boss without him there, but what does he think I'm going to be able to do with my hands in heat resistant cuffs and no way out of the room. I don't think I'll ever get used to people being that scared of me. Not the Others. Not Lionel's group of Faders. Anybody. Still, the bodyguard nods eventually. He heads for the door with his colleague and they step outside, presumably to look menacingly at anyone who approaches.

Senator Hammond holds out his hand for his son, and Johnny steps over, taking it.

"Can I play now, Dad?"

"Not yet. I need to tell Celestra and Grayson here about what you can do."

Last time we were here, the senator told us that his son had some kind of talent, but he didn't give us any details. Now, with everything he has said, I can put the rest of it together.

"Johnny?" I say. "Johnny, how is it that you know all about me?"

"I saw you," Johnny says. "I dreamed of you. I dreamed of you, and Grayson, and Jack. I dream lots of things."

I crouch down so that I can look him in the eyes.

"You're still tied up," Johnny says.

I nod. "I guess your dad still thinks that I'm dangerous. What kinds of things do you dream about, Johnny?"

"He has a gift," Senator Hammond explains, not letting his son answer. "Or maybe a curse. He sees things. Most of them come in dreams. At first, I didn't think they were anything important, but then I read some of the intelligence reports about the Others and the Faders, and... well, there were too many similarities to ignore."

"I saw stuff," Johnny insists.

"I know that now, Johnny," his father says, and he looks sad as he says it. Whatever Johnny has seen, it obviously isn't good.

"So you're saying... what?" Grayson says. "That Johnny's clairvoyant?"

Senator Hammond shakes his head. "It's more complicated than that. Clairvoyance would mean seeing things in other places, but Johnny does far more than that. We think... we *know*, that he sees other *times*."

"He can see the future?" I say.

Senator Hammond nods, and at the same time, Johnny winces. He obviously doesn't like being able to see it. That or he just doesn't like what he sees.

"He has nightmares," Senator Hammond says. "He'll wake up screaming, sometimes. Or his head will start hurting, and he'll panic, and he'll start reacting as though things are going on around him. Bad things. Terrible things."

I look at Johnny again. The little boy looks scared, as though he knows what I'm going to ask next. Maybe he does. "What do you see, Johnny?"

"I see you, and I see Grayson. Jack too."

"Yes," I say gently. "You told me that. Is this like a month from now? A year?"

"You're kind of older," Johnny says. "Not like my dad's age, but still older."

"So it's a few years?" I ask.

The senator interrupts. "That's where it gets complicated. We think from other aspects of the visions that what Johnny sees isn't anytime soon. It's the far future, by which I mean thousands of years."

"But I'm not going to be around in thousands of years," I point out.

"You are," Johnny says. "I've seen you."

Senator Hammond nods. "And I've been able to confirm some of his other... experiences. What my son sees is real. Which is why I need him to forget it. There are some things he shouldn't see."

There's something about the tone of that. Something that frightens me. It's like the senator knows that something big is coming, and he's terrified by it.

"What is it?" I ask. "Is it something I do? What happens?"

"It's nothing you do," Senator Hammond assures me. "It would be easier if it were. No, it's something I do. Something that no son should ever see his father doing. He doesn't understand it yet, but he will, and when he does, he'll hate me."

"So that's why you want the fading machine?" I say.

Senator Hammond nods. "So let's hope that Jack hurries up. For all our sakes."

NINE

After that, the bodyguards blindfold us again to take us back to the apartment room. I guess it's not as bad as the tiny cell we started off in, but even a nice prison is still a prison, as I'm reminded every time I try to use my cuffed hands. I look in on the bedroom, and I see that there are clothes laid out there. Senator Hammond obviously wants us to be comfortable. That, or he wants to make sure we look that way for Jack and his father when they come here.

It's hard thinking like that. It's hard being in the middle of a world where practically everybody is lying, and you don't know who to trust. I mean, yes, that's a pretty good description of the average school cafeteria, but the stakes here are a bit higher than whether the in crowd likes me.

"Fresh clothes?" Grayson says. "Great. In that case, I'm going to take a shower and get changed. These clothes have been through far too much in the past couple of days."

That's true. He wore them for the assault on the Others' base, he was wearing them when I almost burnt him alive, and now he's had them on continuously for at least a day and a half. Not that my clothes are in much better shape. Grayson grabs the clothes left for him and hurries off to take a shower, leaving me there to look through the rest of the clothing that has been laid out. There's a nice silk dress for me that reminds me of some of the things I wore when I was modeling as part of my cover ID with Jack.

It isn't long before Grayson comes out of the bathroom. And he looks incredible. His hair is still wet, and he's wearing jeans. Just jeans, leaving his chest gloriously bare as he dries his hair with a towel. When did he get muscles like that? Somewhere in the last few months, it's like someone has flicked a switch and he's gone from "cute looking boy" to "muscular sexy man" just like that. He even smells nice. Clean soap smell on just washed warm skin.

Grayson smiles over at me. "I so needed that. I don't know how you managed to stand being around me that long without a shower."

"I must be used to it," I say with a laugh. I pick up the dress left for me. "I'll be back in a minute."

I head into the bathroom with it, and start to get changed. There's just one problem. I can't get my existing clothes off completely. Not alone. Which means I'll need Grayson's help. Do I really want that, after the footage Senator Hammond already has? But then, what else can he do that's worse? And Grayson has already seen me in my underwear. When we were together, as boyfriend and girlfriend before I was faded, he's seen less. I make my decision.

"Grayson, I could do with some help in here."

He's still shirtless when he comes in. I hadn't expected that, but it's too late now to turn back. He helps me off with my current clothes, finally resorting to tearing the t-shirt when it won't go past the cuffs. There's something rough, almost exciting about that. He's so close I can feel how warm his skin is. And his breath brushes slightly against my skin just so that it's like a gentle touch. Thankfully, the new dress has straps that tie over the shoulders. Grayson steps behind me and ties those in place gently, his fingers barely brushing my skin. He zips the dress up slowly, but doesn't make any move to step away from me.

Eventually, I have to turn around. I have to look at the broad expanse of his chest, and force myself to look up into his eyes. He's so quiet as he stands there in front of me, barely touching, his eyes staring into mine. There's so much desire there. So much need.

"Celes..."

He doesn't say more, but just kisses me. That close, I can smell the scent of the soap he's just used. I can taste him on my lips in the moments before his kisses drift down to my neck and I arch my back allowing him more access. His kisses down my neck becomes hungrier, and I pull him closer. I don't even stop him this time, though I know I should. Then I came to my senses.

"Grayson, we..."

He stops that thought with another kiss, then pulls back. "You've said that I'm in your dreams."

"Dreams of the future," I say. "We're both older, and you're there beside me. Always there."

"Dreams like Johnny has dreams?" Grayson asks. It's such a deceptively simple question, but I don't know how to answer it.

"You're asking me if I see the future?" I ask.

Grayson shakes his head, running his hands through my hair. "I'm saying that if you do, and you see us together... well, maybe this is meant to be. You do love me, don't you?"

He kisses me again, putting his arms around my waist and lifting me, carrying me back into the apartment's bedroom. He tosses me lightly onto the bed, and I lay there, staring up at him. Am I really going to... are *we* really going to...

The door to the bedroom flies open so hard that the bang of it against the wall sounds like a thunderclap. I look around, and so does Grayson. When I do, all I can do is stare. Jack's there. He's there, in the doorway, dressed from head to toe in black, with a black suit, a black sweater under it... even deep black shades that reflect everything in the room without showing his eyes. Everything, including me laying there on the bed with Grayson half undressed in front of me. Jack's expression loses its blankness for just a fraction of a second then, and what I see there hurts.

"So the video file was true."

"No, Jack," I say, scrambling to my feet.

"All the effort I've put in trying to find a way out for you without having to fade the kid, and this is what you're doing behind my back?"

"It's not what it looks like," Grayson says.

I wince. No one says that, do they? Because saying that is almost like admitting that something happened. Except, what else can we say, because it's really *not* what it looks like. I wouldn't have let anything happen. At least, I don't think I would.

The worst part is the way that Jack's expression goes back to something blank and emotionless. He doesn't react. No, that's not right. He doesn't *show* his reaction. Even so, I know how hurt he has to be.

"Come on, we don't have time to talk about this. We need to get out of here, preferably before anyone gets hurt. Go past me and head down the hall. There's another Fader there who will show you the way out."

That's so brisk and businesslike. Pure Jack. Grayson grabs a shirt and puts it on before heading past him.

Grayson stares at him for a second or two, but in those shades Jack is wearing there is just his reflection, and Grayson goes. I know I should do the same. I stand up and start to hurry out, but Jack puts a hand on my arm, taking off the sunglasses so that I can see the pale blue of his eyes. I'm expecting hate there. Anger. Not the love that fills his expression in that moment.

"I wish I could have gotten here sooner," Jack says.

I swallow. "Jack...Gray and I..."

"Later," Jack says, cutting me off. Somehow, I don't think he means it. He doesn't want to talk about this. Not now. Not later. Not ever.

"Jack..."

"My priority is to get you out of here safely, Celes. We need to focus on that, and I can't do it if we start talking about what happened here."

"What about Johnny?" I find myself asking.

"Johnny?"

"That's the name of Senator Hammond's son," I say.

Jack shrugs. "He'll be safe now. Hammond can't fade him without our help."

I shake my head. "It isn't that simple, Jack. He has a talent. A talent like ours. Well, more like yours. He can see the future."

"Like I do?" Jack sounds surprised by that.

I shake my head. "Johnny can do much more than that. His father says that he can see things in the far future. Like thousands of years. That's why he wants to fade him, to get rid of that gift."

Jack looks at me. "He can really see that far ahead?"

I nod. "We have to get him out too. His father's determined to fade him so that he won't see something he does in the future, and it's obviously big, whatever it is. Johnny might be able to tell us what is going on."

Jack pauses, and I know that he's trying to work out what to do.

"Please, Jack. He's just a kid."

Jack nods. "All right. I'll try to find him and get him out." He pauses. "I missed you, Celes."

"I missed you too. Jack…" I go to kiss him, but he holds me back with his hands on my arms.

And through that moment of contact, heat pours into me. I've felt this once before, in the Others' headquarters. There's something about Jack's touch that resonates with the power inside me, driving it to levels I simply can't manage alone. I look down at the handcuffs designed by Senator Hammond's scientists, and they melt. They simply melt. All that heat resistant material gives way in the face of our combined power like it's butter.

I know I should run down the corridor then to join Grayson and the Fader assigned to getting us out, but I can't. I was attracted to Grayson just now, but he isn't Jack. We don't have this kind of connection. There's something more between the two of us. Something that makes me more just through his touch. And I love him. I love him so much that I'd do anything not to hurt him.

Jack sighs, and then kisses me. It's a sweet kiss, a gentle kiss. It's not about passion, or somehow claiming me back as his. It's about showing me that he loves me every bit as much as I love him, and that moment makes me glow. Literally. Light spreads around us as our powers combine, and it's an effort to pull back from him. I rub my wrists, trying to ignore the marks of the cuffs there.

"You need to go now, Celes," Jack says. "I want you to know that I love you, though, and I'm not giving up on you." He looks down at the ruins of the handcuffs. "I think it's pretty obvious we have far too much chemistry for that. I'll see you once we get out of here."

I shake my head. "I'm coming with you. Johnny knows me better than you, and I've spent more time in this place. You'll need my help if you're going to get him out, Jack. You know that you will."

Jack looks like he wants to argue about that, but I cut him off before he can.

"Where would you prefer I was?" I ask. "Out there somewhere with Grayson, or right by your side helping you?"

Jack pauses, but it's obvious that he knows I'm right. After several seconds of hesitation he nods.

"I shouldn't do this," he says. "The priority is your safety."

"Ignore the priorities," I say. "Let's concentrate on what's right. Do you want to leave a little boy able to see the future with a father who's so determined to stop him doing it he wants to fade his memory?"

Jack shakes his head.

"Then come on," I say, and step out of the room.

TEN

We leave the room where Senator Hammond has been holding us and head out through the hallway outside. There are rooms on either side, all with the kind of sliding security doors on the cells. Those don't appear to have locks, just buttons to open them. I guess Senator Hammond isn't too worried about people being let out, and I know from having spent the night in one of them that there aren't any controls on the inside.

Jack presses one of the buttons and a door opens. We don't step inside, because after the way Grayson got trapped with us it doesn't seem like a good idea, but we do glance around. It's another apartment, similar to the one that they've been keeping me in. It's large, well furnished, and empty. Is it intended purely as a comfortable prison? It seems unlikely that anyone would go to that much trouble. So maybe there *is* a way to get the doors open without help, and this is just a place for Hammond's employees to stay.

That seems to make more sense, especially once Jack starts opening more doors. There are more apartments behind each one, and they're mostly empty. A whole block of empty apartments. The one time we do run into someone, it's the woman who brought food for me and Grayson. Jack spins her to the ground and clamps a hand over her mouth, extracting a zip tie from inside his jacket and using it to tie her hands.

"Now," he says, "I'm not planning on hurting you, but I need to know where Senator Hammond and his son Johnny are."

"Why?" she asks. "What are you going to do to them?"

"We're not going to do anything," I say. "We're trying to help Johnny, here."

"He's such a sweet boy," the woman says. She swallows. "The senator will be angry I spoke to you."

"You don't have much of a choice," Jack points out, in a cold voice that I know he's putting on deliberately to scare her. At least, I hope he is.

"Please," I say, partly because I've watched too many cop shows, and I know how the good cop bad cop thing goes, but mostly because it seems like the right thing to say. The woman looks over at me.

"They'll be on the top floor. The senator keeps an apartment in the penthouse, and Johnny's always nearby."

"Thank you," Jack says, and then gags her with a length of duct tape also taken from inside his jacket, leaving her there as we go. I know it's probably the best thing, because we don't want her raising the alarm, but I guess I'll never get used to the clinical, efficient way Jack can be when he's on a mission. I guess that's because I haven't been brought up to be a Fader.

Then again, if everything in the last few weeks is anything to go by, my life is a lot more complicated than I ever thought it could be.

Jack and I look around some more. Now that I know we're looking for a penthouse, the layout of the place makes a lot more sense. It's a skyscraper. It's obvious once I get the chance to see it all. It's just that I've been blindfolded for so much of my time here.

"Did you see this place from the outside?" I ask.

Jack nods. "It's right at the edge of a town, with 'Hammond Industries' down the side in big letters. I guess the senator doesn't believe in secret bases."

"He probably thinks that he doesn't need to hide that much," I point out. "If you're keeping industrial secrets anyway, then adding in a few cells to keep troublesome kids in isn't going to be too difficult."

"No," Jack says. "I guess not."

"Was it hard getting your dad's help for this mission?" I ask.

"He wasn't there," Jack says, "and I couldn't take the risk of him saying no. It was easier just to find a few Faders from the old Locations and put the mission together myself. Quicker too, and I knew that we couldn't afford to waste any time. With a man like the senator, I didn't know what he'd do."

I can't help thinking back to the images on that video file. "Well, I guess we both know now. Let's get Johnny and get out of here."

Jack nods. "You realize he might not want to go?"

I hadn't thought of that. To me, it seemed obvious that anyone would want to get away from a guy like the senator. That anyone would want to get out of a place where they're trying to wipe your memory, but Jack's right. Senator Hammond is Johnny's father, and he obviously cares about him even if he has a seriously weird way of showing it. So even if I know Johnny doesn't want to be faded, there's still a chance that he won't want to come with us.

"What do we do then?" I ask.

Jack pauses for a moment, and then he says what I think we're both thinking. "If he won't come willingly, then we might have to take him anyway. He's not old enough to understand the implications, and I'm not letting the kid be faded."

"So we kidnap him?" I ask. I want to be clear about it.

"We can't leave him here, Celes." Jack moves along the hallway, trying more doors. "Not when they're going to do that to him. And if you're right about what he can see..."

I want to ask if this is about Johnny or about how useful he could be to the Faders, but I don't. I don't need to, with Jack. After what his dad did to him after his mother's death, this is always going to be about Johnny.

We find a stairwell and head up. It's a long climb, but we're both running by then, at the kind of speed only we can. We cover the stairs faster than an elevator would have, quickly reaching the top floor. There's a hall there, with two doors for suites. We stop at the first of them, mostly because Jack puts his hand out to make sure I don't go in. It's then that I hear the people talking in the room beyond. One of them is Senator Hammond, while the other... I know that voice, because it has threatened to kill me more than once. What is Richard, Grayson's father, doing there?

"Scott, take Johnny through to the lounge so that I can finish talking to the doctor here," Senator Hammond says.

"Will I get to see Celes and her friend again?" I hear Johnny ask.

"Maybe if their other friend brings what I need. Go with Scott now, Johnny."

I start to panic, because it seems obvious that someone is going to be coming out of the door in front of us any second, but Jack just pulls me back against the wall beside the door, holding me flat. The door opens, and one of the senator's bodyguards, the one who knocked me unconscious, leads Johnny from the room. He doesn't even glance our way, though Johnny does. Thankfully, the small boy doesn't say anything. He just smiles.

On the other side of the door, the conversation continues.

"It is vital that we get hold of the machine, Richard," Senator Hammond says.

"So you've said."

"Because it's true, and it's time your organization recognized that. Unless Doctor Cook can rebuild the machine for us, or supply us with another, the world, and our future, is in grave danger."

I press closer to the doorway, trying to hear more of what's going on.

"I tried to recover the machine at Location Six," Richard says. "Then I tried to capture Sebastian Cook, and I believe he would have been able to replace the machine had he not escaped with the aid of his son, the girl, and the other Faders."

"And your son, Richard," Hammond points out.

"Yes." There seems to be extra tension in Richard's voice then. "Tell me, Senator, why exactly do you want the machine? It can't be just for fading that boy of yours."

"You don't think I care enough about my son for that?"

"I don't think that the fate of the world hangs on it," Richard points out.

There's a pause. "Clever, Richard. All right. It doesn't make that much difference now, and I guess it at least lets me point out that you and your group have been working on the wrong assumptions about the machine all along."

"You'd better have an explanation for that," Richard says. I know that tone. The last time he used it around me, he was promising that he'd kill me.

"Don't make threats you can't back up," Senator Hammond says. He's obviously less worried about Richard than I am. "As for the machine, the fading is just part of what it does; a feature designed to allow travelers to adopt appropriate identities when they arrive."

"What do you mean, 'when they arrive'?"

Senator Hammond laughs. "I'll be surprised if you believe this, but I'm convinced the device allows for travel through time. As much as I wish things were different, it is how my son came to me. How yours came to you too."

Jack pulls me gently away from the door. "We have to go," he whispers.

I know we do, so even though I want to hear what the senator knows about the future, I follow him across the hall to the room Johnny and Scott the bodyguard went into. We pause by the door, then Jack hits the button to open it. The room on the other side is the entertainment lounge Grayson and I spent so much time in. Johnny is there playing a video game, while the bodyguard is standing there watching the door.

Jack steps forward and hits him before he can even begin to respond, using the same speed that got us up the stairs. Because he isn't set for the blow, Scott can't roll with it, and his head snaps back, his eyes rolling back in his head as he crumples to the floor like a falling tree. After the beating he gave me and Grayson, I don't have a lot of sympathy for him.

Johnny turns around, faces us, and slowly smiles. "Jack, finally. I was wondering when you'd get here."

That is *not* something I'd expect a seven year old kid to say. The shock must show on my face, because Johnny jumps down confidently from his chair and hurries over. "I'll tell you, the accuracy of that device of ours is all over the place. Finding you has been almost impossible."

Again, that sounds strange. The voice is a seven year old's, but the words just *aren't*.

"You're probably wondering what's going on," Johnny says. "Well, let's start with the obvious. The last time I saw you both in the same place, it was thousands of years in the future. Or possibly will be."

I look at him for a long time. "You aren't an ordinary seven year old boy, are you?"

Johnny smiles. "That's the best part. I *am* seven. I'm also as old as either of you. Probably older, in terms of my memories, because I haven't had them taken from me." He looks back and forth between us. "Maybe I should explain."

ELEVEN

"It's kind of hard to explain," Johnny says. He looks at us, and it isn't the look of a little kid. There's too much intelligence in it, or at least too much knowledge about the world. It's subtly wrong, like seeing someone in clothes that are obviously designed with someone else in mind.

"You saw Jack in your dreams?" I ask. I know we might not have much time right then, but I have to ask. We have to know what is going on here. Especially if it might mean that I finally get an explanation about why so many people seem to want me dead.

Johnny shakes his head. "I did, but it's not that simple. My dad thinks I see visions of the future, but it isn't like that."

"Then what is it like?" Jack asks. He sounds slightly disappointed. Maybe that's just because he was hoping to meet someone else who can do what he does. At the same time though, he sounds just as curious as I am about what

Johnny has to say. He can obviously see just as well as I can that there's something very different about the young boy.

Johnny goes to sit on the big armchair in the center of the room. It's far too large for him, but at the same time, it kind of seems right for him. "Do you know me, Jack?"

He says that like they're old friends, even though Johnny isn't old enough to have old friends. Jack looks at him, and I want to ask how Jack could possibly know the young son of a presidential candidate, because that doesn't make sense, but Jack nods.

"You... there's something familiar about you."

"Just like there was something familiar about Celes? About Grayson?"

Jack nods. How could Johnny have known that?

"I don't get this," I say. "I mean, you're just a kid. But you don't sound like a kid."

"I'm a kid," Johnny says. "I'm seven years old. At the same time, I'm also a lot older."

"So how does that work?" I ask. Nothing about this makes sense, yet it sounds like I'm finally about to get some answers about what's going on.

Johnny looks over at me. "I don't see visions of the future, Celes. I just remember it. It's all jumbled up, so sometimes it's like I'm just a kid, and sometimes I have decades of memories, and sometimes I'm both. That's hard."

"So what do you remember, Johnny?" I ask, moving to crouch beside the chair to bring myself down to eye level. Then I stop myself. I'm treating him the way I would a small child, but if what he's just said is true, then he isn't. Or at least, it's far more complicated than that.

"I remember you, Jack, Gray, and me. Only we're all about the same age, and none of us are kids. We... work together, I think."

That sounds familiar. I find myself thinking of my own dreams. I've never been sure what they meant, or how they could be true. "Where do we work together?"

Johnny doesn't look sure, and for a moment, he sounds more like a kid again. "There's an office. A big office, like my dad's. Not the one here, the other one, up in Washington."

"You mean that you remember us being something to do with the government?" Jack asks, and Johnny nods.

That's a strange thought. What would we have had to do with the government?

"I've been seeing a lot of the same things," I say. "But if it's true... *how* can it be true?"

"We travelled through time," Johnny says, briefly sounding older and more confident again. "We travelled back, one by one, using the machine."

"We travelled through time?" Jack repeats. He doesn't sound convinced. "Are you sure that you didn't just dream all this, Johnny?"

"Why would you remember me then?" Johnny asks in return.

I nod. "It fits with my dreams, Jack. I remember... I remember one where I was insisting on being sent back somewhere. On going after someone who'd left."

"What do you mean?" Jack asks.

I try to think back to the dream. It seems like so long ago now, except that if Johnny is right, then it isn't. It's something that hasn't happened yet. "Someone I loved was lost. They'd used a... a machine, and they were gone for a while. People were trying to talk me out of going after them. They said it was too risky, but I went anyway. I loved them too much."

I look at Jack, meeting his eyes. I know that we're both thinking the same thing in that moment. I reach out to take his hand, and for a moment there's no power leaping between us. It's enough that I'm holding onto him, and he's holding onto me.

"You, Jack," I say. "It must have been you."

"I want to believe that," Jack says. "I *do* believe that there's something special between us. I felt it from the moment I was assigned to protect you. I knew that you were always going to be more than just someone to keep safe, Celes. It was like I'd already known you for a lifetime."

"Maybe you had," I suggest. That's a thought it's hard to wrap my head around. What if Jack and I have already known one another for years? What if... no, there are so many 'what if's that if I start to think about them all, I'll never stop.

"Jack went first," Johnny says. "He went first, and he landed first, which is probably why he's the oldest of us here in this time."

"I'm not sure I understand," I admit. It feels strange, asking such a small child for an explanation. "Why would that make Jack older? Why are you so young? Why are any of us younger than the ages I keep seeing in my dreams... I mean when I remember?"

"It's the way the machine works," Johnny explains from his armchair. "At least, I think it is. Living people can't survive the journey back, so the machine kind of just takes them apart. It stores everything about them, and then it rebuilds them."

"You mean like one of those teleport devices on sci-fi shows?" I say.

"Except that this would be real," Jack says thoughtfully. "That would explain why the fading machine can rewrite memories."

Johnny nods. "It needs to, because your memories, your personality, they're what make you who you are. It does that, and it makes a body for you from your DNA, only when it does that..."

"...it makes you as a baby," I say. It's the only explanation that makes sense right then. I guess it says a lot about my life right now that an explanation featuring devices that build people up out of nothing and give them their memories makes sense.

"It's a flaw in the device," Johnny says. "I think... I think we didn't know about it until after we started sending people back, and then once we realized, it was too late."

It seems strange that something like that could happen. That a device like that might be used again and again without knowing what would happen. Whatever happens in the future, we must have a good reason to send people into the past without testing the device first.

I realize then that I've accepted it. I've accepted that I'm from the future, and so is Jack. I've accepted that I've come back through some kind of time machine. That seems like a lot to take in, but some part of me has already recognized it as the truth and gone with it. It's almost the same as the way I seemed to know who Jack was almost from the moment of meeting him.

"So Jack arrived first, and he's the oldest," I say. "What about the rest of us?"

"I don't know everything," Johnny says. "There are parts I don't remember. I know Jack went first. I know you waited for him, Celes, until you knew he'd forgotten the mission. After that..."

"I followed him," I say, knowing that it's true even as I say it. "I knew I might not be able to get back, and by then we knew what traveling would mean, but I went anyway. I wanted to find a way to bring him back."

"Even though no one had done it before," Johnny adds. He looks from me to Jack. "Then Grayson went after you, not long after you'd gone. I remember trying to stop him, but he wouldn't listen. He said that just because he advised you, that didn't mean he had to *listen* to advice."

Jack seemed to be considering all that as much as I was. He looked carefully at Johnny. "Does this mean that you followed later?"

Johnny nodded. "Years later. I don't remember much about that part, but yes. It's also why I remember more, I think. My memories are fresher, and when I saw Celes with Grayson yesterday, it reminded me of who I really was. Before that, even I thought I was just a kid who could see visions. But seeing them there like that... I'd recognize them anywhere."

"And we've ended up in the same place," I say. "It's kind of a coincidence."

Jack shakes his head. "Not really. Senator Hammond is interested in the fading machine through Johnny. The same is true of my father and Grayson's. It's that need to know what is going on that has brought us here."

"Maybe," I say, but I can't shake the feeling that there's more going on than that. "But there has to be a reason why you came back here in the first place, right? So what was it?"

Jack shakes his head. "I don't know. I get the feeling that there was something, but I don't know what it was. There's just... a gap where it should be."

"That happens to a lot of people," Johnny says, standing up. Like that, it's harder to think of him as anything but a little kid, because he barely comes up to my waist. "They come back with the idea of changing the timeline, but the fading machine messes with their brains so much that they don't remember what they were planning on doing. They get caught up in the lives they have here, and those kind of layer over their memories, so that eventually there isn't anything left. They're just people living out their lives."

I guess I shouldn't feel too bad about that, since nothing is actually happening to those people, but I *do* feel bad for them. What would it be like to have your identity completely wiped out? It would be like the real you being dead, wouldn't it? Well, from the sound of it, I guess I'd know.

"But Jack and I didn't lose those memories completely," I say.

Johnny shakes his head. "You didn't, and your powers have started to come out, which means that you might be able to complete the mission you came back for."

"What mission?" I ask. "And who are you, Johnny? I know you're just a kid now, but who are you in the future?"

Johnny opens his mouth to answer that, but Jack interrupts by turning to face the door as it starts to slide open. We've left it too long. We're in a room with one way out, and people coming in. We're trapped.

TWELVE

A couple of men step through the door, dressed in the suits of heat resistant fabric Senator Hammond's men wear. I start forward, but Jack is already moving, almost faster than I can follow. He traps the hands of the first man to enter the room, slipping an elbow past his guard so that the man only just manages to bear the brunt of the blow on his shoulder. Jack throws a fast series of punches, forcing the other man back as he tries to defend frantically.

I throw myself at the other man. With the heat resistant clothes he's wearing, I won't be able to burn him completely unless I manage to grab the exposed skin of his head and neck, but I'm not sure I want to do that anyway. With the bodyguard who knocked me out when I was first here, throwing energy into him hurt and stunned him. That's all I need here. I need to buy Jack time.

So I push into the second of the men, drawing up as much energy as I can, then putting it out through my hands where they grip his coat. He makes a sound of pain, jerking like I've just hit him with a stun gun, trying to throw a feeble punch that I block easily. He obviously isn't quite as tough as Scott was, because he isn't able to fight through that pain to hurt me the same way.

Jack is still fighting the other man. For a moment, he seems to falter, moving back under a flurry of punches, elbows and knees. Yet I see that none of them are getting through. He sees each one ahead of time, and reacts so fast that he parries it easily. So the only reason he's moving back must be...

His opponent doesn't see the trap until Jack swings to the side, pulling the other man around after him. His foot sweeps out along the floor to send his opponent tumbling from his feet. The guard tries to rise, but Jack brings his fist down sharply on the base of the other man's skull, and he collapses into unconsciousness.

Then he's over beside me, helping me with the man I'm using my power to stop. Jack isn't scared of my power, so he just moves forward and hits the guard I'm holding three times, in a swift flurry of punches that sends him slumping to the floor.

"Come on," I say, looking at Johnny. "We should get out of here before..."

Jack puts a hand on my shoulder, and I can see he's still looking at the door. "Put your hands up, Celes," he whispers.

"What? Why?"

When he does it though, I do it too, and just in time. Half a dozen men come in holding sub-machine guns, spreading out so that they can cover us both easily and standing there with the kind of rock solid steadiness that suggests I really shouldn't move. Senator Hammond and Grayson's father, Richard, follow. Richard is dressed the way all the Others do, immaculately in a dark suit. His hair is greying, and he isn't quite as broad shouldered as his son, but I guess now any resemblance between them is a coincidence. Certainly, they're nothing alike when it comes to personality.

Senator Hammond looks at us almost sadly. "Jack Simple. I was expecting you to come back with the means to reconstruct the fading machine, not to try to mount some kind of rescue operation."

"Then you obviously don't know him very well," Richard says. He gestures to us to lower our hands. "Celestra. I wish you had the sense to keep out of things."

Like I believe that he cares what happens to me. Or anyone else for that matter. "I'm not the one who goes after innocent people," I point out. "I'm not the one who goes around having people killed." I look around at the men with the guns. "Why? I haven't done anything."

"You will though," Senator Hammond says. He moves around the room to stand close to his son. Richard follows him. "Right now, Celestra, you might not seem like a threat. You even seem like a perfectly nice young woman."

"But?" Jack says.

"But if our information is correct," the senator continues, "then Celestra here is potentially the most dangerous human being on the planet."

"Assuming that you can still call things like her human," Richard adds.

Senator Hammond shoots him a sharp look. "Her humanity is not in question. It is the threat she poses that is the problem."

They're talking about me like I'm not there. Like I don't matter. I've had enough of that. "What threat?" I demand. "You think I'm so dangerous because I've burnt people? Every time, *every* time, they were trying to hurt me first. It was self-defense."

"Most of it wouldn't even have happened if your men hadn't been trying to stop her because they thought she was so dangerous," Jack points out. "It becomes a self-fulfilling prophecy."

Richard shakes his head. "You think it's as simple as a young woman who can burn people? If that were it, she would be a minor threat, no more than that. What matters isn't what she has shown she can do so far. It's what she is going to do in the future."

Senator Hammond joins in. "If Johnny is right about it, then who you are, what you do, potentially affects so much. And that's the part that makes you dangerous."

"If I'm so dangerous," I counter, "why not just kill me? You've had me here for days. You could have killed me anytime."

The senator doesn't look happy about that. "I'm not in the business of killing people."

"Richard is," Jack says.

"Well, he isn't in charge here," Senator Hammond says.

Grayson's father's expression twitches just slightly at that. He obviously doesn't agree. That, or he doesn't like being reminded.

"Anyway, it isn't that simple," Richard says after a second or two. "The same things that make you so dangerous also make you potentially very valuable."

"You didn't seem to think that before," I say. I note that the men with the guns still haven't lowered them. I guess that talking won't make them lose their concentration enough for us to get away, though Jack doesn't look like he's about to do anything anyway, so maybe that isn't his plan. I hope he *has* a plan.

Richard doesn't seem bothered by anything I have to say. "Before, I thought that you and those like you were of alien origin. That meant that the danger you represented outweighed the potential benefits. Now that we know where you're really from though…"

"It changes things, knowing that Celes and I are human?" Jack asks.

"Of course it changes things," Senator Hammond says. "It means we aren't fighting off some kind of alien invasion, for one thing."

"It means that there are things we can learn," Richard corrects him. "Alien technology or physiology wouldn't be of that much use to us as a species. You have to understand that technology never exists on its own, it's part of a wider collection of connections, ways of seeing things."

"In other words, you wouldn't be able to understand aliens," I translate.

"Not enough to get anything useful from studying them," Richard says. If I've made him angry, it doesn't show. "But you, you aren't aliens. We know that now. We got signals from you, but that's just to do with the energy you generate, and that isn't alien. It's just advanced."

Richard actually looks excited about that, like I'm his favorite new toy. "There are people in this world who can already do things with energy. There are people who can light up light bulbs, or channel energy through their bodies without being hurt, or take massive electric shocks. People dismiss them as tricksters or freaks, but they aren't. They're the start of an evolutionary path."

"A path that leads to you," Senator Hammond says.

I look over at Johnny. All this time he's been silent, but he won't even look at me. All signs of those memories that made him seem older are gone, leaving just the sense of a little boy as he sits there in his too large chair, looking at his father.

Whose side is he on? I have the sense that I know him, but I still don't know from where. In fact, almost everything we know about the future is stuff that he's told us, backed up with just a few fragments from my dreams. He could be anyone, playing any kind of game, and we'd have no way of knowing until it was too late. Or he could just be a little kid with too many memories floating around in his head, trying to make some kind of sense of them.

"For now," Senator Hammond says, "let's get you back to somewhere secure."

Richard nods in agreement, and some of the men start forward. They're his men, then, rather than the senator's. Jack raises his fists, moving in front of me, but that just means that the guns come up again.

"We'd prefer both of you alive," Richard says, "but if necessary, we will make do with just the girl."

I put my hand on Jack's arm. "Don't, Jack. It won't help."

Jack looks at me, nods, and allows the men forward. They bring out handcuffs similar to the ones I've already burnt off.

"Those won't help," I say. "They didn't work."

"They'll slow you down," Senator Hammond says, "and having you here will allow us to work on other things. We'll learn."

One of the men clips the cuffs onto me, behind my back. Then they lead us out into the corridors, to an elevator rather than the stairwell we used to come up, taking us back down. At that point it hits me that I've ruined our escape. If I hadn't told Jack about Johnny, we could have been out of there and long gone by now. If I hadn't insisted on going with him, then at least they wouldn't have captured me.

Yet I can't imagine ever leaving Jack behind like that. In fact, if what Johnny has said is true, then I've crossed time itself so that I don't have to leave him behind. And we've gained something out of it, because we've learned more about how we ended up here. We've learned things that we might never have learned if we didn't come back to try to get Johnny out as well.

Yet it has cost us too. The guards lead us back to the apartment space I shared with Grayson, pushing us inside. Hammond is there, his arm around Johnny's small shoulders.

"You'll be safe and comfortable here," the senator says. "So long as you don't try to escape again, you can even stay together."

Beside him, I see Johnny's lips move. The words are easy to make out, because there are only two of them. "I'm sorry."

I'm not sure what to think. What do those words mean? Do they mean he betrayed us? Or is he just sorry that he wasn't able to do anything to help us escape? Maybe it's something else completely. Whatever it is, we won't find out any time soon, because the door to the apartment slides shut behind us.

THIRTEEN

Almost as soon as the door shuts, Jack turns to me, looking me deep in the eyes.

"Shall we start by getting those cuffs off you?"

"What did you have in mind?" I ask, and I get an answer almost immediately as he kisses me, his mouth moving passionately on mine. "Mmm!" I manage to say before melting into his kiss.

I feel the flash of energy rising up inside me in response to Jack's kiss, the touch of his hands on my face. It burns up through me, and it takes an effort to send it down through my hands, because right then, all I can think about is Jack. I do it though, and I feel the pressure of the cuffs on my wrists fall away as they melt.

"That's one way to do it," I say, when he pulls back.

"One," Jack agrees, "but I could have done it plenty of other ways. I kissed you because I wanted to, Celes."

"Well, I didn't think you'd done it just because it was the best way to generate heat between us."

Jack smiles. "I think we generated plenty of that. I missed you in the time it took to get back and put the mission together. I wanted to show you how *much* I missed you." He's holding my face between his hands, and leans in to kiss me again, so thoroughly my toes curl and I kiss him back with everything I have.

"You weren't gone that long," I say pulling back for air.

"Maybe not long enough," Jack says, looking serious for a moment or two.

"What do you mean?"

"Maybe if I'd stayed away longer, I could have planned the rescue in more detail. I was in such a hurry to get you out of here after seeing you and Gray together in that video that I just grabbed the first Faders I could persuade to help and came over. That isn't how you mount a mission in a fortress like this if you want it to succeed."

"You got to me," I point out, but there's something about the way he said it that's worrying me. "You do think the others got out okay, don't you?"

"You mean Grayson?" Jack asks, just a little bit sharply. The trouble is, that's what I do mean. Grayson went with the other Faders because that was meant to keep him safe. What if it has put him in more danger, though? I know I can't say that to Jack.

"About the pictures Senator Hammond sent you," I say instead.

Jack turns away from me, stepping over to the apartment's small kitchen. "I don't want you to remind me about that, Celes. If I do, I can't focus on what has to be done. I know you were with him before you were with me, that you really didn't break it off with him because of your fading, but it still feels like I was punched in my guts. It still hurts. And the worst part is that I'm still drawn to you regardless of it. I can't help it, whatever time period we're in. I can't help loving you, wanting you."

"Is that so bad?" I ask, moving closer to him. "Look at me, Jack. Don't just shut down and walk away. Really look at me."

Jack spins, staring at me with an intensity that has nothing to do with anger. "What do you want from me, Celes?"

"Everything. Right now though, I want you to believe that I didn't deliberately set out to hurt you with Grayson."

"You kissed him, though."

I nod. "I kissed him back when he kissed me. We went through a bit when you were gone. We were knocked senseless, and I had to rely on Grayson to do the most basic things because they made me feel so helpless, so weak. I was vulnerable, Jack, and yes, it was the wrong thing to do. I wish I could take it back, but I can't. Gray and I have been together for so long before you came along, and things weren't really resolved, and I was having these dreams..."

I can practically feel the tension in Jack. Or maybe it's in me. I don't know. I want to fight with him. I want to tell him that he's being unfair by blaming me, except he *isn't* being unfair. All the time I was with Grayson, I was trying to convince myself that everything was okay, and that it didn't matter, being that close to him, but it did.

"Most of what's on the footage isn't how it looks," I say. "Grayson helped me out with getting washed, because I couldn't get the cuffs off to do it myself."

Jack swallows. "I guess I should be grateful that he doesn't generate enough heat with you to melt them," he says. He still doesn't sound happy, but I guess I can't have it both ways. I'm the one who asked him not to shut me out, and to let me see some of what he's feeling. If I don't like that, it's on me as much as him.

"What about the kiss, Celes?" he asks me softly. "Was that some kind of camera trick too?"

It would be so easy to say yes, but I can't do it. I can't lie to him. I shake my head.

"If you tell me that it was all Grayson, I'll believe you," Jack says. That's the part that makes me feel ashamed of what happened. It's not the hurt or the anger that Jack had before. It's the way he's willing to turn around and try to find a way to set it all aside, because he just cares that much, loves me that much.

And because he cares that much, I owe him the truth. "Grayson started the kiss," I say, "but I kissed him back. I should have seen it coming too. We were packed together in this place, and I could see that we were getting closer, but I didn't draw a line there. I tried to, kind of, but I didn't stop it."

Jack winces slightly, and I can see his face sliding into that carefully neutral expression that he uses so much. I reach out, putting my hands on his face.

"Don't, Jack. Please don't. Let me know what you're feeling. I know it has to hurt."

"It's..." he let's go of his control, and in that moment, I can see just how hurt he is by it. How vulnerable he is about his love for me. It's not anger. It's not resentment. It's just a deep kind of pain at what has happened.

"Oh, Jack," I say, reaching out to wrap my arms around him. He's held me so many times when I've been afraid, or hurt, or unable to cope, so I hold him. I hold him to try to show him that I'm there for him too. That I'll always be there for him. After all, if my dreams are anything to go by, I always will be.

He holds me too, for more than a minute. When he finally pulls back, he looks around the apartment with a professional eye. I take a moment to look too. It's the same apartment I was in with Grayson, so nothing has really changed. It's modern and elegant, with the sofa and the TV, the doors leading through to the bathroom and the bedroom.

"It's kind of tacky," I say, "putting us in the same place I was in before. It's like they want to remind us about Grayson."

"Maybe," Jack says. "More likely, this is the only room they have stocked with food and ready to go. Plus, it makes the surveillance easier."

I'd almost forgotten that, if they used cameras to get footage of me and Grayson, those cameras would still be there. "So we have to assume that they can see and hear us?"

Jack nods. "I'm not too worried about that. They'd spot us in the corridors if we left anyway. Besides, there are some things that I want the whole world to hear."

He moves to stand in front of me, and the way he looks at me then is so intense. "I want you to know that I love you, Celes. I love you, and I'm willing to fight for you. For us. I'm not going to let anyone take you away from me. Not the Others. Not some senator. Not... anybody."

He doesn't say Grayson's name, but I know it's what he means.

He kisses me gently then, planting a second kiss on the tip of my nose when he's finished. "Johnny says that you came back for me."

I look around. "I guess that makes us kind of even. I mean, you came back for me too."

"You followed me through time, Celes. I don't remember it like you do, or like he does, yet, but I can... it's like I can feel the memories in me, like I'm some kind of deep pool, and they're swimming about near the bottom. I don't actually remember them yet, but it's like every time we touch, they swim a little closer to the surface."

"Then we should be touching a lot more often," I suggest, half joking.

Jack smiles. "That's just what I was thinking. I was also thinking that we should get out of here soon, but those two are almost the same thing."

"What do you mean?" I ask.

By way of an answer, he kisses me one more time. This kiss is as hard and as passionate as anything I've had from him before. He kisses me like he plans to keep on going until we both forget to breathe, and his hands press me tightly to him while he does it. I don't even hesitate; I just kiss Jack back as completely, and as thoroughly, as I can.

I feel the first stirring of the energy between us then, growing into something bigger. I kiss Jack's mouth hungrily, wanting more of him in that moment than I have before. Jack's the one who keeps control of the kiss though. His hands find mine, his fingers intertwining with mine as his lips tease me, moving over my mouth, my jaw, my neck.

The power in me rushes to the surface in each spot he kisses, and I can't blame it. Right then, I want to be as close to Jack as I can be too. We kiss, and I know then it's not just about doing what we have to in order to bring out the power that is glowing around us. Jack's kissing me because he wants to, desperately, as though his life depends on it. Because I'm as important to him right then as he is to me. The fact that energy *is* glowing around us both, so bright that I'm sure I wouldn't be able to look at it without my talent, is just a very useful byproduct.

Jack moves back from me, catching his breath. "Try the door."

"Are you sure about this?" I ask. "Before, in the cell, it didn't work, and these doors will be as strong."

"Trust me, Celes," he replies, "if you can melt their handcuffs, you can deal with a door."

I nod, knowing that he has to be right. He has to be. I move over to the door, putting my hands against it, right against where the locking mechanism has to be. For a moment, the material around the door flares as it tries to resist the power I'm putting through it. Then it just… disintegrates. There's so much heat that most of the door is blasted apart in a rush of power, leaving a hole in it where the lock used to be. Part of the frame is gone too. It's easy then to just push the door back, sliding it back into the frame, and leaving the doorway to freedom wide open.

"I wasn't expecting it to work that well," I say.

Jack smiles. "You're always full of surprises. Now, we should go, because there will be guards along in a minute."

He's right, of course. We've just broken out while on camera. There will be people running to stop us even now. I reach out to take Jack's hand.

"Let's get out of here, then."

FOURTEEN

The weirdest thing as we start to make our way through the building is just how empty and quiet it is. I'm expecting alarms, guards, and a constant running battle. Jack obviously is too, because he moves through the place warily, not running, but staying ready to fight.

"Should we try for Johnny again?" I ask. "I know we have to get out of here, and I'm not sure whose side he's on, but the thought of him being faded..."

Jack nods. "We can't let it happen. We have to find out what he knows. But we can't stop to talk this time. We go in, we grab him, and we get out. Even then, it probably won't be easy."

I'd kind of guessed that. If I were Senator Hammond, I'd triple the guards looking after his son, or keep him right by me, or something. "If it's too hard..."

"If it's too hard, we'll have to leave him," Jack says, "but since nobody seems to be reacting to us breaking out, hopefully we'll have the element of surprise on our side."

"You mean because nobody would think we'd be stupid enough to try to break Johnny out twice?" I ask with a smile.

Jack returns it. "Exactly."

We head on up through the building, and it's still almost eerily quiet. We make for the lounge room, ready to fight if we need to, but it's empty. We try the room across the hall. That's a large suite with views out across the small town that the Hammond Building is on the edges of, in an industrial park. I look out at the place. If the people out there knew what was going on in here, how would they react? Looking down at it, I'm not sure. It's such a small town. The kind of town, in fact, where almost everybody works for the big local company, and where they wouldn't want to hear anything bad about it.

Just looking down at the business park around the building shows me that it's almost as quiet and empty as this building is, too. So maybe there aren't even that many people in the houses I can make out in the distance. The whole place has the feel of a town that was mostly abandoned a while ago. That, or one that is still waiting for people to come to fill it up.

I'm still thinking that when a figure walks out of the adjoining room. I recognize the woman we tied up before, and she obviously recognizes us too, because she opens her mouth to scream. Jack manages to clamp a hand over her mouth just in time.

"It wouldn't do any good," Jack says, before removing his hand. "Now, I didn't get your name last time."

"Janine."

"Hi, Janine. Now, I want to know pretty much the same things as before. Where is Johnny?"

"He went with the senator," Janine says. There is a sofa identical to the one in the apartment we've just come from. She sits down on it.

"And where did the senator go?"

Janine looks around, as though trying to think of a way out of the situation, but all there is there is a slightly more opulent version of the rooms below. I step into her eye line.

"You have to tell us. There isn't much time."

"He took his guards and those... other people, and they all left. There's just me and a few guards on the lower floors, and I haven't heard anything from them since they went to deal with some kind of disturbance."

"That will be Grayson," Jack says. "Did the senator say where he was going, or what he was planning to do?"

"Just that I needed to be ready to take care of Johnny when he came back, because he'd probably be confused."

"They've gone after the fading machine," I say.

"Which means that they're going after my father," Jack points out, "because the original was destroyed with Location Six. We have to get out of here now, Celes."

We don't bother tying Janine up this time. There doesn't seem to be much point, with the building so empty. Instead, we race down through it, down stairwell after stairwell until we arrive at some kind of lobby. There are doors at the end, made of what looks like tinted glass. Through them, I can see...

"It's Grayson and the Faders," I say. "They made it out."

Jack nods, though he doesn't look as happy to see Grayson as I am. We head over to the doors, which have an opening mechanism beside them. It's locked, but that doesn't seem to matter once I put enough heat directly through the mechanism. It whirls briefly, and then the doors slide open.

We step out and the Faders all turn to look at us. They're heavily armed, and they half-raise their guns before they spot who we are. Grayson looks like he wants to hug me, but he looks over to Jack and he stops short.

"Celes, Jack, you made it out."

"So did you," Jack observes. "But you're still here."

"We wanted to wait for you to get out," Grayson says. "We wanted to secure your exit, but then we found we couldn't get back in."

"Couldn't you just break the glass doors?" I ask.

Grayson shakes his head. "They aren't glass. They're like a see through version of the stuff on the rest of the place. We couldn't break them. We tried shooting them. We even tried the kind of entry explosives they use to blow holes in walls. Nothing worked. We were planning on waiting for someone else to come out so we could go back inside."

"You mean you haven't seen anyone come out other than us?" I ask. That doesn't make sense, if the senator has left.

"Hammond must have other ways out," Jack says. "Though this place... it's strange. It's so fortified, and so shielded against all kinds of energy, but it's so luxurious inside. It's almost like it's designed to keep the world out while the people inside are fine."

"It's like that entertainment lounge," I say. "There's no way that's just for Johnny. Or for us."

Jack nods. "That's not important now though."

Grayson looks over to him. "Why? What's happening?"

Jack explains. Not just what the senator is planning to do next, but also what Johnny said about us, the presence of Richard, and how the fading machine might be a lot more than we'd previously thought. He explains that we're from the future, and about the abilities people there seem to have. When he's done, he looks around at the Faders.

"I know none of you were expecting that, and I know that some of you might find it hard to accept, but it's the truth. I just hope that for now, at least, you'll keep going with this mission. I told you because I think you all deserve to know."

The Faders don't reply. Mostly, they're too busy looking shocked. Even Grayson seems surprised to hear all of it.

"I guess it makes a kind of sense," he says at last. "I mean, it explains why the three of us should end up meeting like this. It explains why... why I feel..."

He doesn't finish that thought. There are too many people watching. *Jack's* watching. But so am I. I know what Grayson means. He's made it very clear how much he feels for me.

"None of that matters right now," Jack says. "What matters is that Senator Hammond wants to fade Johnny's memories."

"He said that was to keep memories of something he was going to do from him," Grayson says.

"It might be," Jack shoots back, "but it also means that we won't have access to the knowledge of the future in Johnny's head. They're trying to get to a fading machine, and we have to beat them there."

"Location Ten," one of the faders says. "They're heading for Location Ten?"

Jack nods. "Which is why we need to get out of here as soon as possible."

As soon as possible turns out to be just a few minutes. During them, Grayson slips off to the side of the group, and I follow him.

"Before, I wanted to say-"

"I know," I say.

"I didn't believe in love at first sight until I saw you. Now though... well, I guess it isn't first sight after all."

"I'm still with Jack, Grayson," I say.

Grayson shakes his head. "I won't give up."

"Even if I loved Jack so much I followed him through time?"

"Well, why did I follow you?"

I don't have an answer for that. Thankfully, I don't need one, because our extraction helicopter arrives. It takes us up, and we fly for what seems like an impossibly long time. So long I lose track of where we're going, except that there seem to be swamps below us. Are we in Florida?

The helicopter heads for a space in the swamp that seems like just a patch of water near some trees. It lands, and it's only when a boat comes out of the trees to meet us that I realize that this is our destination. Jack hops down into the boat, lifting me down after him, and I can see the look on Grayson's face as he does so, but the boat is already moving. I'm guessing it can't take more than a few of us at a time.

We sit in the boat as it takes us over to the trees, and there, I find myself surprised. On the other side of the trees are a series of low buildings, each one obviously reinforced and camouflaged until it must be like they aren't there from above.

"This is Location Ten?" I ask Jack.

Jack shakes his head. "This is Location Nine."

"But why not go to Location Ten?"

"Because I asked him to bring you here when he went to rescue you." That's from Sebastian Cook, Jack's father, and one of the leaders of the Underground. I'd thought that he was still hundreds of miles away, in Location Four. The surprise must show on my face, because Jack starts to explain.

"When I went back and told them what happened, and my suspicions about who might be involved he and Jonah evacuated. A compromised Location can't be used. They went here, taking the rock we found."

"Talking of which," Sebastian says, "Jonah?"

Jack's uncle comes out of one of the building, his limp as noticeable as ever. The two men don't look much like one another apart from their graying hair and age. Jonah is much more rugged, looking like the farmer he was pretending to be at Location Four. Sebastian still dresses more like a successful businessman.

"Good," Jonah says, "you're back. We've managed to do more analysis of the rock, using what we know about the two of you. I should probably tell you what we found, Celestra. You too, Jack, if you have time."

Jack shakes his head. "I have to go. It turns out that Senator Hammond, the presidential candidate, is working with the Others. He wants to fade his son, and that means he'll probably be heading to Location Ten to do it. That is where we put the one fading machine that wasn't destroyed in Location Six, right?"

Sebastian nods. "He must be desperate. I told him no. I've... learned my lesson when it comes to fading people that young."

He looks away. Jack doesn't say anything.

"But you seem desperate to stop him, Jack," Jonah observes. "It isn't just the boy is it? What else?"

"Johnny knows things," I say. "Things about the future that seem very important. Thanks to Johnny, we're convinced that me, Jack and Grayson all came back from the future, and that we did it for a very specific reason. We just aren't sure what."

"And if he's faded," Jack continues, "we never will."

FIFTEEN

Before Jack can go anywhere, Jonah speaks up. "Jack, I think that we have something you need to see first. Celes and Grayson too."

Which means we have to wait for Grayson to arrive on the small boat, but that only takes a minute or two. Once he does, Jonah leads the way into one of the low buildings hidden in the swamp. It reminds me of Location Six, because almost the moment we get inside, there's an elevator leading down.

"It was hard work to keep this place from flooding," Sebastian says as he follows his brother in, "but it was worth it."

The elevator comes out in a large room below, which is largely empty, with doors spaced evenly around the walls and video screens between them. Those are familiar enough, but what makes me pause is what's on the walls. There is material there that looks identical to the stuff that was in Senator Hammond's building. As an experiment, before I can even really think about it, I send a flicker of power into the nearest wall. Nothing happens.

Jack obviously sees it too, because he turns to his uncle. "What's this?" he asks. "Why do we have the same material here that the senator had?"

"My guess would be that he somehow obtained intelligence relating to our facilities," Sebastian says. "Though how, I'm not sure. Even among the Faders, this place is highly secret."

"Which should mean Lionel isn't a problem," Jonah adds.

I'm glad about that, but this place still seems strange. "Why build it if no one else knows about it?" I ask. Then I ask the other obvious question. "Why are there all these secret places around? Senator Hammond has that building of his, the Others have their fortress, the Faders have all their Locations... and they're all these big, reinforced bases. Why not just a normal house somewhere?"

Jonah sighs. "That's where it gets complicated," he says. "I can only tell you about our bases, but my stepsister, Jack's mother, had nightmares for years. They were dreams about the same thing. An explosion so big everything was destroyed. At the time we thought that it meant an explosion on whatever world she had come from."

"So we built places like this when we started to investigate what we believed to be the alien technology," Sebastian continues. "We wanted to protect ourselves from anything on a similar scale, stay out of sight, and be able to defend ourselves from the Others."

"As time went one," Jonah takes over, "we realized that she had a talent for seeing things that hadn't happened yet. That's when we started adding the best heat resistant materials we could to this Location."

"You made a bomb shelter," Jack says.

"Exactly. The other bases will withstand a lot, but they were designed as much for defense as anything. This is even more secure against blasts."

"That still doesn't tell us how Senator Hammond had the same material," Grayson says.

He's right, but I can think of one obvious solution. "Johnny. Johnny must have told him about the material. He must have remembered it from his past... our future."

Jonah looks at me. "There's someone else like you?"

His brother cuts him off. "The important thing right now is the fading." He turns to me. "By experimenting with the power source we found in conjunction with our files on you, we've worked out why we weren't able to fade your memories, Celestra. A block had been placed on your memories, protecting them. Or rather, protecting what is underneath."

"What do you mean?" I ask.

"Your personality, your identity, seem to have been faded into place."

That makes sense, I guess. After all, Johnny said that the time machine used fading as a way to imprint the children it created with their personalities. He also said something else that makes sense. "You're saying that there are layers of memories I don't have access to yet, aren't you?"

Jack moves close to me, putting an arm around me.

"We did find something," Jonah says. "A memory where you are you, but not you."

"Whatever it is, I'll be there for you," Jack whispers. "Remember, you've already seen so much of the future with your dreams."

Grayson moves to the other side of me, his hand on my shoulder. Standing like this, with both of them beside me, I almost feel like someone else, like there are memories of moments just like this stirring within me. "Remember the nightmares you had?" Grayson says. "The ones where you were yelling for people to take cover. It's the same thing. You need an explanation, Celes. I know you."

It's true. I need to know what's going on. I take a breath and look over to Sebastian. "Can you show me the memories?"

Sebastian nods. "I think so. We have the data. It was simply a question of realizing what we had. Follow me."

He leads the way through one of the doors dotted around the large entry room. On the other side of it there is a smaller room, with seats at one end and a large projection screen at the other. In front of the screen there is a complex looking projector linked to a computer, with a box beside it. Sebastian goes over to the box, lifting out a data chip and connecting it to the computer while the rest of us take seats.

Images play on the screen. These are bright. So very bright. And familiar too. I may not remember what's happening here, but somehow I know that these are my memories. The camera is looking out of my eyes, in an office that seems to be too brightly lit, as though it's a particularly warm summer's day. I look around, seeing a desk, a computer, and some expensive looking furniture. In this memory, I'm in an office, and it appears to be an important one.

There's a man standing beside me. He's in his early thirties, wearing a dark suit that I know from my brief modeling career looks expensively tailored. He's tanned, muscular, with a leaner face and handsome, but I recognize him instantly. Grayson. The real Grayson's hand returns to my shoulder as we watch.

There's something even stranger than that though. In the footage, I look down at the computer screen, and I catch sight of the reflected image there. It's me. It's definitely me, but at the same time it simply *isn't*. I'm older, the same age as the version of Grayson that we all just saw, with a harder expression that says something serious is going on. Or maybe that's just how I look all the time in the future.

There is sound to go with the images. That surprises me. The last time I watched something like this, the images were mute.

"Celes," Gray is saying, up on the screen, "if we're right, this is the moment that changed Earth as we know it. As you know, we found the old chip in one of our digs, in a Fader Location."

"I know," I say, and it's strange hearing my voice, but not quite my voice, coming out of the speakers. "I was there, remember? Did we get enough off it?"

Grayson nods. "It's ancient, but the footage is still good. I'm surprised it lasted this long and has such high resolution."

"But did we get what we're looking for?" I ask, and the on screen version of me sounds impatient.

"It's all right, Celes, I want to track him as much as you."

"I know," I say up there, "I'm sorry. You're certain of the time he faded to? I just hope he got close enough to accomplish the mission."

The older version of Grayson nods. "He's resourceful. The best we have, but the odds... I think we would have noticed if he'd succeeded, and you know no one has returned after being faded back. I'm worried that he might have forgotten."

"We've been waiting too long," I say.

"You want to send more people after him?"

The older me shakes her head. At least, I assume that's why the image on the screen moves back and forth. "That won't change anything. You know that the side effects of the machine are too much for most people. We tested it."

"John had good results," Grayson says.

I hear the other me sigh. "We need John here to contain the disease. And after him, I tested the best."

Grayson's hands are on my shoulders on screen. "You aren't seriously thinking about doing this yourself?"

"Who else is there?" the older me demands. "Who else can accomplish the mission? We've sent enough people back to know what happens to those who aren't strong enough. The machine's re-write of their personality locks their memories away too deep. Maybe I can get to them where other people can't."

"And what if you're wrong?" Grayson demands. "You could go back, lose yourself, and we'd still see everything here destroyed."

There's a shift in the images on screen. A different memory? No, I realize, just the computer screen playing footage of its own. Footage of people out on the streets. Footage of the explosion. The heat. The light. The terrible, terrible light...

On the screen, Grayson is holding her. Holding *me*. And I can see the glow around me. It's so familiar now, the sight of my body wreathed in heat and power, but the older Grayson holds me without being harmed.

"If only people could have escaped," she says.

The older Grayson shakes his head. "They didn't have shelters. And they couldn't have seen it coming."

I can hear the sound of myself crying then, and in some ways, it's a relief. It means that the version of me up there is still me. Still totally, definitely me.

"If I leave him there, he dies," she says up on the screen.

"I know," Grayson says. "Which is why you can't go. He knew the risks. We can't lose you too. I-"

"I don't care about the risks." The camera shifts, and it's obvious that the older me has stood up. "I can't leave him there, Grayson, but it's not just that. I can't let this happen. If we have the power to change this, and we

- 149 -

do nothing, then it's like killing all those innocent people ourselves. You know it is."

"I know I can't let you go."

The older me pushes back from him. "I know how you feel about me, Grayson, and you know how I feel about him. You also know that this is my decision to make. You can't stop me from doing this. It's what I have to do."

Grayson shakes his head. "You're too important here, Celes."

"Here I can't do anything," the older me says. "Here, I'm just holding things together until they collapse completely. I'm important *there,* Grayson, because I can stop this. John can handle things here. He can help…"

The footage stops, fading into static. I look over at Jonah, but the scientist shrugs.

"I'm amazed we got that much."

"But what does it all mean?" I demand.

"I know."

I look around, and Jack is standing. The look in his eyes is haunted, and he's paler than usual. "I know. I know what it means." He looks at me. "Celes. President Celestra Caine. I remember."

SIXTEEN

Jack takes me by the shoulders, kissing me. I can practically feel Grayson's eyes on us, but right then I don't care. Jack certainly doesn't. He kisses me until I think he might never stop, only pulling back when Sebastian Cook coughs pointedly.

"I remember, Celes," Jack says. "I remember everything. At least, I think I do. The mission. You, me, Grayson and John. All of it."

He looks around the room almost like he's seeing it for the first time, and his eyes fix on Grayson. He moves over and claps him on the shoulder. "You came after me with Celes, buddy. I wouldn't have thought you would. I'd have thought you'd have found a way to keep her there and be happy. I know you've always had a thing for her, even though Celes and I are together."

Grayson looks at him like he can't quite believe what he's hearing. I'm not sure I can either. "Are you trying to tell me," Grayson says, "that we're *friends* in the future?"

Jack nods. "Best friends. We have been for years. We went to the same college, then to the Academy together. Celes too. She was the strongest of us, of course, with the best abilities. Not to mention the highest marks. But then, I guess that was pretty easy to see coming. She always was smart as well as beautiful."

He moves back to me. "It's strange seeing you like this, Madame President. I can remember the older you at the same time as seeing you like this. With you so young... it's like reliving college."

He kisses me again, and it's another good kiss, but this time I pull back.

"What is it?" Jack asks.

"It's just... which version of you are you at the moment?" I reply. I need to know. The future me might be in love with the future Jack, but right now, if he's a completely different person, then that complicates things.

"I'm me," Jack says, taking my hand and putting it on the center of his chest. "I'm always me. I'm exactly the same guy who walked into this room with you, and who took you out of your life months ago. I haven't changed,

Celes. The whole way the fading machine works means that I can't change. The personality it imprinted in me is *me,* just the same, in the past or the future. I remember more, that's all.

"So what do you remember?" Grayson asks. "And why do you keep calling Celes 'Madame President'?"

Jack shrugs. "Because she is. Or she will be. President of the United States, not to mention our best hope of containing the crisis in the last days of humanity."

"You remember that?" I ask. "You know what's going on?"

"I know some of it," Jack says. "I may not have all the detail... I'm not sure I ever knew all the detail, but I know enough. I know what I'm here to do."

"And what's that?" Sebastian asks. What must it be like for him? What must it be like, with a son he thought of as his own, whom he brought up as his own, but who is really the result of a futuristic form of time travel? What must it be like, confronting the fact that everything he thought he knew about his own son is wrong? Pretty much the same as the way I'm feeling about Jack right now, I'd guess.

Jack looks grave again, the way that he did after seeing the footage his father and uncle had recovered from my head. "I'm here to prevent the end of the world." He looks round at me and Grayson. "I guess we all are."

"The literal end of the world?" I ask.

Jack shrugs. "You saw it, Celes. You saw the great disaster. The Apocalypse. Millions... *billions* of people dying. And that's just the first phase of it. The initial disaster has knock on effects. It kills so many people, but it isn't quite the end of the world. In our time though it looks like we *are* heading for that."

"Which is why we came back," I say.

Jack nods. "Us and so many others. They all tried to change things, and they either got the timing wrong, or they weren't able to overcome the effects of the fading machine enough. Who knows how many of them there are walking around the world, believing that they are just normal people, with normal families? In fact, with the way the fading machine works, they *are* normal people with normal families."

"What do you mean?" Jonah asks. I can hear his scientist's interest in the advanced technology the fading machine offers.

I explain a little based on what Johnny told us back at Senator Hammond's place. "People can't travel through time directly, but the machine effectively re-creates us in the past, as babies."

"Which means that we have to grow up as normal," Jack says. "The machine imprints us with our personalities, but could you imagine being a newborn baby with the full knowledge of everything that was going to happen? It would drive you mad. An infant brain isn't developed enough to deal with the full adult self, so that part is... locked away is the wrong way to put it. Put into storage, maybe? Which is where the problems start."

"I'm not sure I understand," Sebastian says.

Jack gestures vaguely, as though trying to capture something impossible. "The memories are meant to come out, but in most people, the imprinting of the base personality is too strong. The lives they live here get in the way so much that all those old, locked away memories stay like that. At best, they get dreams and senses of things being subtly wrong. The implanted memories of their future selves don't come through."

"My fading you can't have helped," Sebastian says, the guilt obvious in his voice.

Jack shakes his head. "I think that's part of why I couldn't cope after what happened."

What happened. The death of the woman he thought of as his mother, murdered by the Others when they believed her to be something evil and non-human.

"I had too many memories," Jack says. "Too much trying to come through when I was so upset."

"I'm sorry," Sebastian says.

Jack shakes his head. "That doesn't matter now. What matters is the Apocalypse. The one now, and the damage it causes in the future."

"Will we be safe here?" Jonah asks. "We built this Location because we knew there might be dangers, from your mother's dreams, from the way the world has been changing, but will it be enough?"

I nod. "It was in the footage, remember? In my buried memories. We found the information in one of the old Locations, so it must have been enough to protect things at least a little. It sounded like it was pretty hard to find though."

Jack nods. "I remember it was hard to pin things down. Hard to find what we needed. Even I went as much on a guess as anything. We knew what the event was, but we couldn't be precise about when it happened."

"Why not?" Grayson asks.

"Remember how far ahead it is that we're from," Jack points out. "Thousands of years. In this time period, it would be like trying to pinpoint one specific event in the Bronze Age, or a Roman town."

"They remembered Pompeii," Grayson counters.

Jack shakes his head. "The rest of the world was left after Pompeii."

I think that's the first time I really get how bad what's coming is going to be. "You mean that there won't be anything left?"

Jack hesitates. "I don't think anyone really knows for sure, but it's bad, Celes. People have been predicting the end of the world for as long as there have been records, and this is the closest it has been. This world is devastated, and the world of the future... that's worse. When I left..." He doesn't finish that.

I haven't really thought about that. How bad would things have to be to get him to go? To get him to give up everything he had... *we* had in the future? What is it that humanity is facing there? Whatever it is, it's obviously bad enough that it's on a par with what's coming in this time, and that sounds terrifying.

"Tell us the mission, Jack," I say. "I don't think I can remember it alone. There's still a block in the way. What are we back here to do?"

"We're here to stop it," he says. "There are signs of things getting worse, of heat rising and natural disasters increasing, but everything we've done points to a single moment that triggers the end. The Apocalypse isn't an accident. People cause it. Specific people."

It's easy to guess who. "Senator Hammond."

Jack nods. "He's one of them."

"He said that he wanted to fade Johnny to stop him remembering something he was going to do," I say. "It's this, isn't it? He causes the Apocalypse."

"That's what I think," Jack says. "That's what we all thought, when I left. I was given a list of people who were part of it, and his name was at the top of the list."

"Who else is on it?" Grayson asks.

Jack shakes his head. "That isn't important now. If I'd remembered a few years ago, maybe it would have made a difference. Now though, there isn't time."

"You make it sound like the end of the world is coming tomorrow," Grayson says. Jack doesn't answer.

"It isn't, is it Jack?" I ask. "It isn't literally tomorrow?"

Jack shakes his head. "Not tomorrow, I don't think, but it *could* be days. Remember that I left before we found the exact date. That's why I arrived early."

I think back to the images that I saw in the footage from my memories. There wasn't a date there either, but it's obvious that I know it. If I could just get through to the memories that are buried in me, we'd know. Jack seems to sense what I'm thinking, because he puts a hand on my arm.

"Even if we knew for sure, it wouldn't change the timescale, and we don't have much time to spare to make you remember. We need to act now, and just trust that you'll remember what you need to as we go."

"So, what exactly is it that we need to do?" I ask.

"The plan used to be simple, but now, I think that there are two priorities," Jack says. "It used to be just a case of stopping this, but now, with it so close..."

"You aren't sure if we can actually do this?" Grayson asks.

Jack shakes his head. "So we need to get as many people to safety as we can. There are buildings that will withstand what's coming. The strongest Locations, Hammond's base."

"It's not enough," I say. I can still remember too much of those images. "Whatever we do, people will still die. So many of them. We need to stop this."

"Which means we need to stop Senator Hammond," Jack says. "Whatever it takes."

Something about the way he says that sounds ominous. "What are you saying, Jack?" I ask. "Exactly what was the mission you were sent back with?"

Jack looks at me for several seconds. "It's simple Celes. I was sent back to kill the people who are going to cause this, before they can kill everyone else."

SEVENTEEN

"You want to assassinate Wilson Hammond?" Jonah asks, sounding shocked. Jack looks at him and shrugs.

"The Faders have killed people before. How many of the Others have I killed, over the years? And I know some of our people have gone out hunting them."

"The Others would have killed us," Sebastian points out. "It was us or them."

"Right now, it's Hammond or the entire planet," Jack says. "Look, I don't actually want to kill him. I just want to stop him. If you can give me a better way, then I'll use it. It's just that right now I can't see one. Can you, Jonah?"

His uncle shakes his head. "I guess not."

"Are you sure this is what we need to do?" I ask Jack.

He takes my hand in his. "I guess this is one of those areas where the you from the future understands better," he says. "There, you've seen everything that's going on, you've made so many hard decisions... it's almost a shock to hear you ask it."

"I *am* asking it though," I say. I'm not going to be pushed into agreeing with Jack just because he's so confident, and perfect, and...

"If we imprison him, he might escape," Jack says. "If we talk to him, he'll lie, or have us killed. If we shut down his plans for now, he'll start them back up again. The world isn't safe with him in it, Celes."

"I don't like agreeing with Jack," Grayson says, moving to stand by the projector, "but put it like that, it doesn't sound like we have a lot of choice."

"I understand that," Jonah says, "even if I don't like it. What I'm saying is that you won't find it easy."

I nod. "Jonah has a point. I mean, senators are going to be pretty well guarded."

"Senators?" Jonah says. "You haven't seen the news? You don't know what day it is?"

I shake my head. I don't know what he means. With everything that's been going on recently, I guess I haven't been keeping up with the rest of the world too much.

"Turn on the TV function," Sebastian says, and Jonah moves over to the projector controls, pressing buttons. Quickly, images come onto the projector screen once again, only this time, they're obviously taken from current news channels. Four of them occupy parts of the projection in a split screen effect. I realize that they're all showing the same thing.

Election coverage.

"But it can't be the elections yet," I say.

Sebastian Cook shrugs. "It is. Probably you lost track with the amount of running around you've been doing recently."

So that's why the news footage showing Senator Hammond promising aid was on TV. It was part of the campaign to make him look good. That, or a commentary on the probable winner, because even a quick glance at the screen shows that he's currently on course for a landslide. He's there addressing party supporters, his wife beside him. One person is notable by his absence, though.

"Johnny isn't there," I say. "They must have taken him off to fade him."

"Then we have to get to him first," Grayson insists. "We'll need to tell Location Ten."

"We have already notified them," Sebastian says. "As soon as I got word from Jack about what was happening, I warned Lionel about the potential dangers."

"Lionel?" I say, not quite able to believe it. "Lionel's at Location Ten?"

"Yes," Sebastian says, "and he should be able to give any of the Others who show up a nasty surprise or two. Why?"

"Didn't Jack tell you what he and his people tried to do to us at the farmhouse?" I ask.

To my surprise, Sebastian nods. "He told us that some of Lionel's people had attacked you, and that you believe Lionel feels that you are dangerous. What you have to understand though is that when you went missing, it was Lionel's people who told us. They would not have done that if they had been involved, would they?"

"It was one of Lionel's people who attacked me and Celes," Grayson counters. "They were trying to kill us. Why would they do that if Lionel was loyal?"

"When you went missing, I asked myself the same kind of questions," Sebastian says. "I looked into Lionel, and it's true that he's cautious where the safety of other Faders is concerned, but I don't believe he would ever do anything to risk Jack's wellbeing, or the organization as a whole."

"So you don't think he's a traitor?" I say.

Sebastian shakes his head. "I think someone has done a good job of making it look that way though."

"Who?" Jack asks that. "If someone were able to make it look like Lionel is working with the Others, then that would mean..."

"That the Faders had been infiltrated," Sebastian says. "I know that. We believe that one of Lionel's people was a double agent. She appears to be dead now."

"Because Celes burned her," Grayson says. "Are you really telling me that you think Lionel is innocent? That he wouldn't have known what was going on?"

Sebastian shrugs. "We didn't, so why should he? I know I've told you in the past that Lionel and I don't see eye to eye on some things, but he is loyal. I've had proof of that loyalty again and again over the years. There is no one better suited to holding off the Others at Location Ten than him, and I won't hear anyone say otherwise."

"I hope you're right," I say. "If Johnny is faded, it could be bad."

Jack nods. "I think we're just going to have to trust that my father is right on this one." He turns to Sebastian. "Will Lionel be able to hold Location Ten against a serious attack? Will the Others be able to get to the machine?"

"It should be fine," his father says. "Lionel called in people from other Locations to help guard the place, so nothing short of an army should be able to get through to the machine."

"That's good," Jack says, his eyes on the screen in front of us. "Because I don't think we'll be able to head for Location Ten anytime soon. I won't, at least."

"What?" I ask. "Why not? Don't you want to get to Johnny?"

Jack nods to the screen. On it, Senator Hammond is celebrating. On it, the words 'opponent concedes election, Hammond victorious' roll around and around across the screen. He's won. The guy who kept us all locked up, who had us beaten up and threatened, who wants to fade Johnny's memories. He's won the presidency.

Jonah does something with the controls for the projector and one of the news reports fills the center of the screen. Senator Hammond... *President* Hammond, is addressing his supporters.

"I'd just like to take a moment to thank everybody here," he says, looking out over the assembled crowd to the cameras. "I'd like to thank all of you for putting in so much hard work in the past few months. I'd like to thank everybody who has helped to get the vote out today, and everybody at home who has voted to make a real difference to this country. I'd especially like to thank my lovely wife for agreeing to deal with the kind of constant exposure that a presidential campaign means, and for seeing just how important what we're trying to achieve is."

Well, yes, I think. I guess the end of the world would qualify as kind of important. I'm pretty sure though that bringing it about didn't form part of his election platform. Though it might have made for some interesting presidential debates.

"Now isn't the time for making promises," Hammond says to the waiting crowd. "I've only just heard that my opponent has pulled out of the race, and in any case, I'd guess that you've all heard far too many promises from me over the past few weeks. Today is about celebrating the success you have all helped to bring about, and about being thankful that the people of our great nation have entrusted me with such a great responsibility. Today is about enjoying this moment."

Hammond's expression turns a little harder then. "Tomorrow though, we'll start working to make the changes that we all need, and that you all voted for. I promise that I will work as hard as you all want me to in order to build a safer, better country. In order to build a future that we can all be proud of. Thank you."

Predictably, the crowd around him breaks into a standing ovation. I guess that's what happens in a room full of committed party supporters. And if I'm honest, I guess that a week or two ago, I wouldn't have been too unhappy to see Wilson Hammond win the election. He came across on TV as a trustworthy guy, with sensible policies and an ability to persuade people that meant things might actually get done. That was before he locked me away, though. That was before I knew what he might be trying to do.

No one speaks when the TV switches off. No one says anything for almost a minute.

"So now he's the president," Grayson says at last. "The guy who's going to end the world is the president."

"We still have to stop him," Jack says.

"Is it just me, or does that feel kind of... I don't know, unpatriotic?" Grayson asks. "I mean, I'm pretty sure that assassinating a president is kind of frowned upon."

"Speaking as a future president," I say, thinking of the footage that Sebastian managed to pull from my memories, "I'm not exactly happy about it either."

"How do you think I feel?" Jack demands in a tone that's a lot more serious than either of ours. "I've spent most of my life keeping Celes alive and safe. I even swore to protect the president, whoever that was. But Hammond... what he's going to do... he has to be stopped."

I nod, slipping an arm around Jack's waist so that I can hold him close. "I know. I know what's at stake. Well, kind of. But this... it's a huge thing to try to do, Jack. It won't be easy. Getting to a senator would be bad enough, but the president is far, far harder. If it goes wrong, you could be killed."

Jack kisses me, softly. Almost like he's saying goodbye. "I know that, Celes. I knew that stepping into the fading machine. I knew that, whether I succeeded or failed, I probably wouldn't be coming back. I thought I had to succeed because it would prevent a great disaster and save our world. Now... now I have another reason."

"What's that?" I ask.

"You're here. If I don't succeed, the Apocalypse will come, and you'll be here. I won't risk that happening to you. I'll do whatever I have to do to keep you safe. To keep us all safe."

"Including killing the president?"

Jack looks up at the screen again. It's blank now, but I can almost see him picturing Wilson Hammond's face. "I'm as patriotic as the next person, but I swore to protect one president. If that means doing whatever I have to so that I can stop another, then so be it."

EIGHTEEN

"Whatever you're going to do," Jonah says, "you had better act now." He presses a few buttons, and the screen shows two images. Both look like they're of the sun, only one is noticeably larger than the other. Not by much, but the difference is there.

"It's already begun," I say.

"Don't worry," Jonah says. "We're in a safe house. The materials here should be able to withstand the increase in temperature. At least assuming that the sun doesn't expand enough to actually consume the Earth."

"We've prepared for this," Sebastian adds.

I shake my head. "But millions of people haven't. They'll die."

"Only if we don't stop it," Jack says, taking each of his guns from his jacket in turn and checking them before replacing them. "Is the chopper re-fueled and ready to fly?"

Sebastian nods. "If it's what you need."

"We have to stop Hammond," Jack says. "He's the key."

I know he's right. I can feel it. This is why I came back. This is what I'm here to do, as much as Jack is. Which means I need to help. I also need to prepare for the worst case scenario.

"We need to get to Hammond," I say, "but we also need to protect people. There is so much space in the Locations, and I can't believe the government won't have other shelters in place too. Hammond and the Others' places show we're not the only ones prepared for this."

Jonah pulls up a screen showing a series of orange dots, scattered all over the world. "As far as I can tell, all these dots represent shelters. Some are ours, but others are run by governments around the world. I suppose people have been prepared for this eventuality for a long time. It's not that surprising when you think about it."

"People have been predicting the end of the world for a long time," Sebastian agrees.

"I don't think any of us actually expected it to show up now though," Jonah says. His face is ashen.

"So the first priority is to get people into those shelters," I say. It seems strange to be taking charge like this, but at the same time, it feels like what I'm meant to be doing. "Can you do it without causing panic?"

"We'll use the Faders," Jonah says. "They're used to being discrete. Even if they're successful though..."

"Not everyone can fit in the shelters," I finish for him. "Millions of people will still die. I know, which is why stopping this is the key. And that's why I'm going with Jack to see Hammond."

"I'm not sure-" Sebastian begins, but I cut him off. I'm not sure where the confidence to do it comes from.

"I am," I say. I turn to Grayson before he can say anything, putting a finger to his lips. "No, Grayson. I need someone to get people to those shelters. Someone I can trust. You're a Fader, and you know how to do this, so it should be you. After all, you were never even meant to come back here."

"You sound like you aren't coming back," he says.

I shake my head. "Don't worry, you'll see me again."

"Celestra," Sebastian asks, "what exactly do you think you're going to be able to add here? Jack is a highly trained operative, but you..."

I laugh. "I'm from the future, Dr. Cook. I know what's going to happen. I know who I am there too. I'm the most powerful person on the planet. Trust me, I need to be there when we try this, and if Hammond won't listen... well, we'll find another way."

Jack nods and heads out of the door, obviously going for the helicopter. I start to follow, but Grayson stops me. He kisses me, his lips jamming against mine in an embrace that's almost bruising in its intensity.

"Stay safe," he says. "I don't think I could stand it if you... if things didn't go well."

"I'll be fine," I promise. "Just concentrate on getting everyone you can into the shelters."

He nods, kissing me again. "I will. I'm going to make sure that your parents and your brother are in one. Johnny too, even if I have to go to Location Ten to do it."

The earnestness with which he says that is almost heartbreaking. Will I really see him again? With the danger of what I'm about to do, I just don't know. "Make sure that Sebastian, Jonah, and I guess even Lionel make it too. The world is going to need them, whichever way this goes. And Grayson?"

"What?" he asks, and it looks like he knows what I'm going to say.

"Make sure you're there too. If I'm not back in time, if I don't manage to stop this, then you need to make sure you survive. You need to find a way back through to the future to try to help there. Don't do anything stupid."

Grayson takes hold of my shoulders. "You're coming back," he insists. "If you don't, then I'll find you, wherever you are. *Whenever* you are. I love you. I always have. I always will."

I kiss him then. I can't help it. "I'll always love you too, Grayson."

I run for the helicopter. Jack is waiting for me, looking impatient. He can probably guess what has taken me so long. He doesn't complain though as we set off.

"Where are we heading?" I ask. "The White House?"

Jack shakes his head. "He won't be there yet, thankfully. He hasn't been sworn in. My guess is that he'll be busy celebrating at his campaign headquarters with everybody else. That, or at his home. We'll find him, wherever he is."

"Will we find him in time though?" I ask.

Jack sighs. "I hope so."

We head for Virginia, and I know the countryside we're flying over, because we've been over it once already.

"We're heading for the town where his headquarters is?" I ask.

Jack shakes his head. "The next town over. That's where his campaign headquarters is, along with his official home. I guess it's close enough that he could make a dash for the bunker if he needed to."

I look out of the helicopter, trying to work out when that will be. The clouds around us are strange, roiling and twisting even though there doesn't seem to be any sign of a storm. Worse, the sky has taken on an orange cast, like the setting sun, only it's too early for that. Far too early. I reach out to touch Jack's arm.

"It's starting."

"We might still have time," Jack insists. "We have to believe that, Celes."

"What I don't get is how Hammond is even causing this," I say. "I mean, this might not be normal, but it looks like a natural disaster, not something man made. And he's only just become president or rather president elect. It's not like he has access to the country's weapons or anything yet."

I'm distracted by things that burn across the sky, falling to Earth in a blaze and seeming to explode when they do so. Meteorites. Ones that glow with energy so brightly I can see them even from up here. I can't help thinking back to the rock we found out in Switzerland.

"How?" I ask. "How can Hammond cause this?"

Jack looks over at me. "You know how this can happen, Celes. At least, you did in the future. These effects are all signs. Signs that Hammond is the one..."

"The one?"

"The One to Bring the End Days. Like I said before, the details are in plenty of mythologies, but when you look in the bible, in Revelations, it's so clear. Someone rises during the End Days and charms his way to a position of great power."

"Like the Presidency."

"He promises peace," Jack says, "but he brings death and destruction. Supernatural occurrences surround him, so that he appears to some people to be a god, but he isn't. He's an agent of evil instead."

That's a lot to take in. "So all this..." I wave a hand as more meteorites come flashing down, seeming to burn the sky as they go "...you're saying that Hammond is controlling this?"

Jack nods "'And it does great signs and even makes fire to come down out of heaven upon the earth before men'. That's from Revelations Thirteen."

I don't want to believe it. It all seems far too fantastical. The idea that the end of the world could be coming now, exactly as set out in the bible... it's too much. Yet Jack's right. The signs are there, and Hammond is right at the heart of what is going on. With that going on around us, we don't have time to waste.

"Hammond's just a part of what is going to come, Celes," Jack says. "There are so many signs in the Book of Revelations, and we know from our research that they happened. They *will* happen, I should say. The false prophet, the Serpent, acquires followers. He brings fire upon the Earth, he takes away religious freedom to force everyone to worship him. He promises prosperity, but just brings plague instead. Hammond has begun to fulfill that role. If we leave it much longer, we'll be too late."

I can't help shuddering at that thought. "We have to stop him, Jack. Whatever it takes."

Jack nods. "That's the plan. That was always the plan. Succeed or die. Either we stop the Apocalypse, or we're caught right in the middle of it."

We're close now. The helicopter pilot brings the craft in for a brief landing, letting us scramble off near a building so covered in campaign banners and posters that it's obvious that we've found the right place. There are people running out of it, along with the buildings on each side. Some of them are pushing, shoving, screaming, so that the chaos of it all isn't far from turning what should be an evacuation into a riot.

Jack and I fight against the flow, making it to the door. There are still people rushing out, and Jack manages to catch the door before it closes, letting us in. It's almost too easy. Hammond might not be sworn in as president yet, but he should have protection around him by now. He should have better security than this. There's something very, very wrong about how easy it has been to get in here, though when I mention it to Jack, he shrugs.

"People are panicking. Panicked people don't remember to do things like locking doors."

Maybe that's it, though it doesn't feel like it. The office around us is mostly large and open plan, with tables set out with phones on them where volunteers have been helping with the campaign. There are signs of a party around us too, with fallen plastic cups and old style party streamers scattered here and there. There's another office towards the back.

"We should check it," Jack says, "but I don't think Hammond is here. Now that things have started, there's a good chance he'll have moved to his shelter. I was hoping to get here before this."

I nod in agreement, but we move forward anyway, opening the office door as silently as we can. We slip inside, finding a small office with a heavy oak desk and leather chair, with TVs set up, all tuned to the news. Hammond is there too. The newly elected president is standing to one side, so that we don't spot him straight away. Just standing there, silently, watching us.

And he's holding a gun.

NINETEEN

Hammond levels the gun at us, then with his other hand, he pulls out a cell phone. He calls a number without saying a word to either of us, the expression on his face not changing even slightly while he does it.

"Honey, something has come up, so it looks like I'm going to be late for the celebratory dinner tonight. You know how these things are just after an election. No, I don't know what time I'll be back, so why don't you go ahead and start without me. I'll get over there when I can."

He hangs up, and now his expression changes, but still not by much. He looks more calmly curious than angry or dangerous, though the gun doesn't waver.

"So," he says, "I doubt that the two of you have come here to congratulate me. How did you get out, anyway?"

I try for my most authoritative tone, aiming for the kind of voice I remember from my dreams, where I'm the one who's president, not Hammond. "Senator Hammond..."

"I think you'll find that it's Mr. President now, young lady."

"President Hammond," I say, "you have to stop. You can't go through with becoming president. You have to step down."

He raises an eyebrow. "Really? Why? Oh, don't tell me, you think that I'm some kind of evil monster set on taking over the world, right?"

I force myself to look him squarely in the eye. "That's exactly what I think you're going to try to do, yes. And I think that in the process, you're going to end up doing more damage than you could possibly believe."

"So you want me to step down?" Hammond says. "All on the word of a teenage girl with a knack for setting light to things? Whatever you can do, you don't have any right to ask that of me, and you aren't even old enough to vote, let alone decide what's right for everyone around you. Why should I listen to you?"

"Because I know what is going to happen," I say. "Jack and I aren't from this time. As hard as it might be to believe, we're from the future. Far in the future. We know what you end up doing here, and we know how much damage you cause. We're here to stop you. To show you exactly what you're about to do."

"I think he already knows that," Jack says, and Hammond smiles slightly. "You do, don't you? You said it when you were going to fade Johnny. You needed him to forget what you were going to do, so you must know *exactly* what is going to happen. Even your safe house... unless you knew, why build it?"

I realize that Jack is right. I'd been hoping that the newly elected president might not understand the consequences of what he's doing, but if that's the case, why build a shelter to protect his family and friends from those consequences? He knows.

"Yes," Hammond agrees. "I know enough about that to guard against the consequences. Further out... well, I don't have a crystal ball, but I do have Johnny. He gave me plenty of information. Enough to know that we would have dangerous visitors. Visitors like you. I've known it for a long, long time."

"How long?" Jack asks. I can see him glancing around the room, obviously looking for a way to deal with the situation. Hammond obviously sees it too, because the gun moves from me to Jack.

"Long enough to get the Others started," Hammond says. "When they were a government division, they were very useful in hunting down your kind. Making sure that meddling visitors couldn't do too much damage. They were so useful, in fact, that when they lost their funding, I was only too happy to use my fortune to fill that gap."

"You mean that the Others work for you?" I say. I hadn't expected that. I'd known they were connected, but this seems insane.

"Oh, most of them don't know it," Hammond explains. "They just know that they have a benefactor who supplies them with money, information, and occasional bits of technology."

"And in return, you just make a few requests?" Jack guesses.

Hammond laughs. "Hardly. By supplying the right information, I don't *have* to ask for anything. The Others do what I want them to, and they think that it's their own idea. It's a far more effective way to run an organization like that, in the long run. If I tried to control them directly, they would only fight against me. Like you."

"We're trying to save people," I say. "President Hammond, I don't care what happens to me and Jack here. This isn't our time. I know though that if you take office, a great disaster will occur in this time, and the knock on effects *will* affect our time. People will die here, but in the future…" memory floods back to me. Memories of the sick and the dying, the comatose and the faces of the doctors who can't help.

"In the future," I say, "there aren't many of us left. We've developed so far, we can do so many things, but we're sick." More memories come to me. Memories of visiting the hospital. Of seeing the children dying. "There's a fever, and we can't stop it. All we could do was look back for the cause, hoping to prevent it at the source. The cause is this moment. The moment when you become president. You bring about changes."

"What kind of changes?" Hammond asks.

I shake my head. "I'm not going to tell you. I'm not going to risk giving you a blueprint to follow. The point is that you have to stop this."

Hammond stands there and shakes his head. "It's too late for that." Then he reaches down to the sleeve of his gun arm, unbuttoning it and pulling it up. There, on his forearm, sits an elaborate tattoo. It's of a dragon, coiled around his forearm like it's clinging to him. "My course has been set for a very long time. It's in me, and I know what I am. For a long time, I wanted to stop it, but now? Now, I know the truth. There is no stopping it. Things are going to be how they were always meant to be for me. But you..."

He stares at me, and I don't know what he sees there, but there's something almost terrifying about his gaze. It's not that it's mad, or evil, or anything like that. It's that it's so calm. So utterly calm as he shifts to point the pistol at me.

"It's not too late to stop you. I think you'll be even more dangerous than I am. I'm sorry."

He pulls the trigger.

As he does so, Jack is already moving, but even he isn't fast enough to stop the bullet that slams into me. I feel the moment when it hits me, passing through flesh like it isn't there. I fall to my knees, pressing my hand over the wound to try to stop the blood that is already coming from it. In theory, if I don't die, then I'll heal, but how quickly? Quickly enough to stop the blood?

Jack is on the new president in an instant, grabbing the gun and twisting it aside, his hand going over the top in a hard punch. Hammond, amazingly, doesn't go down, but starts fighting back, wrestling for the gun while swinging punches with his free hand. Jack has to duck his head down behind his shoulder to stop them, coming back with knees and elbows.

One gets through, a vicious upward elbow strike that catches the former senator on the point of the jaw. He crumples as the blow thuds home, and Jack wrests the gun from him, hitting him with the butt of it so that Hammond falls to the floor, unconscious.

Jack looks over at me. "Are you all right?"

"I'm not sure," I admit. "I think... I think the bullet went straight through, and I haven't died, so I should be able to heal. What about Hammond?"

Jack cocks the gun and points it at the new president's recumbent form. "I came here to do a job. Whatever it takes."

I know in that moment that I can't let him do it. I thought that I would be able to, but here, with him standing over Hammond's unconscious body, I can't. I just can't.

"Jack, wait!"

"Why?" Jack demands, his surprise obvious. "This is what we came here to do, Celes. This is the only way to stop the Apocalypse from happening."

I shake my head. "It can't be. It isn't a solution. You saw Hammond. You heard him. The Serpent is a part of him, but it isn't *him*. Kill him, and how do we know that it won't just move on? How do we know it won't just move on to someone else and use them to take over the world? Hammond is just another pawn here, Jack."

"That isn't what we decided back home," Jack says. "Whatever the Serpent does afterwards, it's in Hammond now. We can't worry about anything else." He sighs. "I'm tired, Celes. I just want to do this and go home."

A thought occurs to me then. One so terrible that I can't bear to think of it. "What if there's no home to go to, Jack?"

"What?"

I swallow as the implications of Hammond's death start to sink in. "Are we sure that I came back to help you? Are we sure I didn't come back to stop you?"

"What?" Jack sounds confused. I can't blame him. "Why would you do that?"

"Because... what if we do change the future, Jack? What does that do to you, to me? To the future we come from? Does it cease to exist? All those people we're trying to save in our time. What if we aren't saving them? What if we're making it so that they never exist?"

"So we just let all this happen?" Jack asks. "Celes, you can't be serious. You're saying that unless we let the Apocalypse happen, you're worried about whether our time will still exist?"

"I thought I came back just to follow you," I say, "but doesn't this make sense too? Are you saying I'm wrong?"

Jack hesitates, but then shakes his head. "It could be a better world in the future though," he says. "One with plenty of people. One where they don't *have* to adapt the way we have."

"One where everyone we've ever known is never born," I point out.

"I know that!" Jack replies hotly, but then stops himself. "This is what we sent people back for, Celes. Are you telling me that you don't want me to do it now? If you are..."

"Yes?"

Jack nods. "I'll do what you want. Whatever that is. I trust you."

The question is, what do I want to do? Jack puts the gun down on the table, and while he does it, I try to think. Does the Apocalypse in this time have to happen? If it does, doesn't that mean the inevitable destruction of our world anyway? The sickness? Maybe someone like me will be born in the future anyway if we change things. Maybe someone like Jack will, too. The trouble is, I can't see a way that they'll meet there. Not the way we did.

Is that what this is? Is it not about the lives of all the people who won't ever exist if Jack shoots Hammond after all? Is it really just about the fact that I love him, and I don't want to create a world where he and I might not exist, let alone meet? And if so, am I really willing to accept the destruction of this past world to keep him? Can I have that on my conscience? Can I have *my* world on my conscience?

This was supposed to be so simple. Now it's anything but. Especially when men burst into the room.

"Get your hands up," one of them orders, making sure his two colleagues have us covered before moving over to Hammond and helping him to stand. "We got your message, Sir."

Message? I realize he must mean Hammond's phone call. It wasn't to his wife after all. Being 'late for dinner' must have been some kind of emergency code. Hammond brushes off the other man and steps over to me.

"You should have let Jack take the shot, Celestra. Leaders can't afford to let their hearts get in the way. They must always do what needs to be done. Like now. Take them please."

One moves over to grab me where I am on the floor, bending over to do it. He gets too close, and I reach up, the power jumping through me as I touch his face. Even wounded like this, it's easy to do. He screams, the bright power of it consuming him.

The other two stare at me, shocked, and Jack moves in that moment. He hits the guard nearest to him, knocking the man to the ground while Hammond reaches out for me. Why would he risk that? Why would he try it when he's just seen what I can do? I don't know, and Jack obviously doesn't want to find out. He moves between us, so that Hammond's reaching hand touches him rather than me.

Energy flares into life around that hand. Bright energy. *Familiar* energy. Somehow, he's doing exactly what I do. I'd thought Hammond was just normal, but he's different. He's like me. Which begs the question of where he's from, because he can't be from this time if he can do that.

Can he?

TWENTY

Hammond's burning energy slams into Jack, but it does not hurt him, any more than mine would. Jack absorbs the power, and Hammond just clings to him in shock, like he isn't expecting Jack to be able to do it. That's obviously one aspect of Jack's powers his surveillance didn't tell him about.

While he's clinging to Jack though, it's easy for the remaining guard to move up behind Jack and strike him with the butt of his gun. Jack might see it coming, he even starts to turn into the blow, but with Hammond holding onto him, he can't do anything about it. As he collapses, Hammond tosses him aside like he doesn't matter.

I throw myself at the guard, my burning power coming to the surface, the pain of my wound easy to ignore now that I'm angry. I reach for his face, but he's smarter than the other one. He grabs my hands, keeping me off him while Hammond wrenches my arms behind my back. From there, it's easy for the guard to cuff me.

"Haven't we proved enough times that these won't hold me?" I say.

Hammond throws me to the ground beside Jack. "They'll hold you long enough."

"What do you want to do with them?" the guard asks. "I can make sure no one finds the bodies. After what they did to Phil, I'd be happy to."

Hammond looks down at me then, and what I see in the next few seconds... I wish Jack were awake, because I just can't believe it. He glows with the power within us, but it's more than that. He actually seems to grow until he's almost touching the ceiling. For a moment or two, spikes of that light form horns above his head, while the glow in his eyes pulses a deep, angry red. His voice shifts too, becoming something deeper, something utterly inhuman.

"The human side of me is foolish. It wanted you dead quickly. I want you to see. I want you to watch everything that happens to the world next, and know that you were not able to do anything to prevent it. I want your arrogance in thinking that you could to bring you to despair."

"You really are the False Prophet, the Serpent," I say, swallowing in my fear. The guard beside Hammond looks at him like nothing is happening. Can he not see this, or is he just so used to it that it doesn't make a difference to him? How could someone see this, hear this, and still work for Hammond?

Hammond smiles then, as though I've managed to amuse him. "*The* Serpent? Oh, I'm just one of them, Celestra. There are many more. We're in the time of deception now, and soon it will be the time of destruction. After that, there will be peace and prosperity for a time, but the destruction that follows that will be even worse. It will seem like the end of the world."

I look at him, and everything we worked out in the future makes sense. We were right about this being the starting point. I hadn't understood how it could be until now, but it is. It's one unbroken chain, disasters setting up disasters, and Hammond knows about all of it. What he's doing now, it isn't just an accident that it causes all that suffering in my time. He's doing it *because* it will cause that suffering.

Perhaps I should have let Jack shoot him after all, regardless of the consequences. I try for him now, lunging up from the floor in an effort to burn him. Hammond just laughs as we touch, my power doing no more to him than his did to Jack. The energy just slides over him, blending with the power that burns around him like some fiery halo. I keep going with it, pushing power into him, but he just shoves me back, and the guard with him slams one swift elbow into my solar plexus, knocking the breath from me. He's obviously wearing the same heat proof stuff as all Hammond's guards, if he can do that without burning.

"You sure you don't want her dead?" The guard asks as I stare up at Hammond with hatred. "It would be a lot easier, that way."

"I don't pay you for what's easy for you. I pay you to do what I want, and what I want is her in the shelter." Hammond smiles down at me, and it's clear that my attack hasn't made any difference to him at all. "How is it going to feel, Celestra? How is it going to feel, knowing that you failed? Knowing that you're safe, while so many other people are at risk?" He nods to the guard. "Get them to the shelter now."

The guard shakes his unconscious colleague awake, and together they lift Jack and me out to a waiting van, which is coated on the inside with the same stuff as the cells in Hammond's shelter. They lift us like we're nothing, tossing me inside to land hard on the wound in my side. It's already closing, thanks to the power I've used, but that doesn't make it hurt less when I hit it on the floor.

There's a small window in the rear of the van, and through it, I can see the sky. More flames come down from the clouds, from skies that are the color of blood. I see a house behind us burning, people running from it. One is trying to beat out flames as they lick up his clothing, another, a woman, is looking back into the house and screaming like someone didn't get out.

That's only the first fire. More follow. Too many more, as flaming rocks fall, summoned down by Hammond. It's starting. Everything that I saw in the footage taken from my memories. Everything that we came back to avoid. It's starting, and all because I was too worried about what might happen to me and Jack to let him end things. I feel tears touch my eyes. What has my selfishness cost the people here?

It isn't a long drive over to the town where Hammond's shelter is. The guards drive up to a secure entrance and then carry us inside, without even asking if I'll walk. They take us back up through the building, depositing us yet again in that secure apartment. They throw Jack's still unconscious form on the sofa, leaving me in the middle of the room.

"You know I could break out of here easily, right?" I say, as they turn to leave. "I've done it before!"

They ignore me, walking out and shutting the door behind them. I guess they don't care if I try to escape. Or maybe they just think that no one would be stupid enough to try it when there is fire raining down from the sky.

I turn the TV on, and find footage from around the world there. Everywhere, the destruction is the same. The fire is raining down. People are panicking. There's worse than that too, because other natural disasters are rising up. There's a sudden flood in Bangladesh, with more than a million people feared dead. There's an earthquake in New Zeeland, a hurricane in Brazil. Jack wakes while this is happening, and he doesn't say anything. He just takes one look around at where we are before watching with me.

"We're too late," he says.

I nod. "I should have let you kill him."

"Yes."

Then Hammond comes onto the TV, and we both stop to watch. "My fellow Americans," he says. "People around the world. Earlier today, I was elected president of this country, and now, it seems that has happened just in time for us all to face the greatest disaster that has ever befallen our planet."

He sighs. "I knew when I campaigned for this role that the world was a harsh one. That people at home and abroad found themselves faced with war and famine, poverty, starvation and disease. Now, it seems that we face a worse threat."

The cameras cut to images of space, where a long plume of fire seemed to be extending from the Sun towards the Earth. The camera in the interview with Hammond looks up towards the sky, and the plume is large enough that the camera can pick it out easily.

"Our scientists have established that this plume will reach Earth in just a short time, meaning that I must now do something I was hoping not to have to do. I must reveal to you the blessings that God has given me."

Hammond raises his hands towards the plume, and it seems to stretch and twist for a moment before vanishing. He glows then. He glows with power live on national television. "You can see the power that God has granted me," he says. "It means that I can protect us from the start of this disaster, but there will be worse to come. I will speak to you all later."

Jack and I stare at the screen while increasingly shocked news commentators try to make sense of what has just happened. Hammond's move is a clever one. He has created a crisis, and now he has presented himself as a savior. It's the kind of thing most people won't be able to believe, though it isn't long before we have an even bigger shock.

The current president comes on TV, reading a statement. Hammond's men are in the background, which could only mean one thing.

"These times are without precedent," he says, "and so I have chosen to take unprecedented action. I have to admit that I can do nothing to protect us from the dangers that have risen up in the world so suddenly, but I believe that Wilson Hammond may be able to. Not only have the people spoken to choose him, but it is clear that God has chosen him as well. As such, I have decided to step down early from the presidency, and allow him to take over the role immediately. I and my team will of course offer him any aid he requires."

I want to shout out at the screen that it's all false. That it's a trick. Yet I know it won't do any good. I've never felt so helpless. Hammond is on the screen now, and it's obvious that he's been waiting for this moment.

"There is no need to panic," he says. "We are prepared for situations such as this. There are shelters in place to protect people from the dangers ahead."

"Enough shelters for everybody?" a journalist asks.

Hammond shakes his head. "Sadly not, which is why I plan to make access to them open and fair. If you wish to be included, please proceed to the local voting areas where you cast your vote today. There, my team will be waiting to allot places. Those who are successful will be tattooed on their hand with a symbol allowing access to the shelters for them and their family. Please note that this is a time of national emergency, so anyone attempting to cheat the system will be dealt with using the full force of the law."

"What about those people who don't get in?" the journalist asks.

"You're worried about yourself..."

"Amanda."

"Amanda, I'm sure you have as good a chance as anybody of getting in. If not, you have seen what I can do. Be assured that I will do everything in my power to make the shelters unnecessary. Simply go back to your home and pray that I am successful."

The screen changes, showing locations for some of the shelters. Jack shakes his head.

"He's set this up to look like God. The people who wear his mark will be saved, while the others..."

"He's going to wipe them out," I say. "He's going to cause the disaster I saw."

The room shakes briefly.

"Probably one of the fireballs," Jack says. He pulls me tightly to him. "We're safe here though. After all, this is Hammond's own shelter."

"I know," I say. "I'm worried about everyone else though. And about why Hammond wants us alive so much. No, not even Hammond. The Serpent in him wants us for something."

"Whatever it is, we'll deal with it," Jack promises. "I just hope that Grayson and the others are deep in their shelter by now."

"I wouldn't have thought you'd have wanted him there," I say.

Jack shakes his head. "He's my friend, Celes. Whatever else there is, he's my friend. We need him, too."

"He went to Location Ten," I say. "He went after Johnny." I put my hand to my mouth. "What if he doesn't make it?"

"He will," Jack says. "And he'll stop them fading John. Though maybe it would be better if they did. Hammond might only be his father in this time, but he's right, hearing that he's the Serpent will change John. It will haunt him."

He slips an arm around me. I don't know what to say to it. I just know that I feel safe there with him holding me.

And suddenly I know more. I can feel the memories coming back to me. Us living together, the way we did in the apartment in New York, only it's the future versions of us. Us arguing over what it could mean if we married, given that I'm the President and Jack's in charge of Homeland Security. People already don't like our relationship, but we're going to go ahead with it anyway. Just as soon as we solve the droughts, and the famines, and… I remember Jack volunteering to go back. I remember trying to talk him out of it. Yet there are still too many things I don't remember.

"What kind of president am I in the future, Jack?" I ask. "What kind of person?"

"You're you," Jack says, smiling as he remembers. "You're always yourself, Celes. You're smart, strong, beautiful… people always feel that you have their best interests at heart, even when they don't agree with you. And to me… you're everything."

He kisses me then, and I know it's true. Past, present or future, regardless of what President Hammond does, regardless of whether the world ends, Jack Simple will always be there for me.

EPILOGUE

How have we come to this? That's the question I keep asking myself. We're meant to be so highly evolved, so much closer to perfection than people were millennia ago. We can do things with our bodies that they could only dream of. We can move faster, live longer, survive things that would have killed any one of them in the past. I can do things that are impressive even by the standards of the people around me. Yet none of it is enough.

I look around my office. The oval office, that ancient symbol of the presidency I hold. How many times has it been rebuilt since the disaster? Yet always to almost the same plan, at least as far as the archaeologists could tell. The materials are different now, because no one these days would ever build in bricks and stone, but even so every time I step in here I can feel the connection to history. This room is closer to the romans now than to the present day, a symbol of something ancient and almost lost.

Yet it's not that my eyes are drawn to. It's the screen in the middle of the room showing the latest figures for the sickness. They're high. Too high. We still haven't found a cure. We still haven't found a way even to make sure that people survive it. We've advanced so far beyond anything the people who first built this room could have imagined, and yet we're still at the mercy of a simple disease.

I sit down in the chair behind the desk. The president's chair. My chair. It feels so lonely and empty without Jack here. I shake my head, knowing that I shouldn't put my personal feeling above the good of the nation. Of the whole world. Yet I think I might have stopped him if I could have done it. I need him here, with me.

I try to distract myself by reading the file that Grayson has left for me. It's the latest theory on how the disease began, trying to pin it down more and more precisely. In theory, if we know how it began, then we can stop it. We can do almost anything now, and time... time hasn't been a problem for a while now. Yet another thing that the former incumbents of my office wouldn't have believed.

Grayson's report is straightforward. He knows that I like that, so he keeps his reports that way. He knows so much of what I like by now. With Jack gone, he's just been there for me. Some days, it's hard to ignore why he makes that effort. He probably thinks I don't know that he's in love with me, but it's Jack I want right now. Jack I'd give almost anything to see again.

Focus. I have to focus.

The idea is simple enough. In the early twenty first century, there was a nuclear disaster on a scale people couldn't have comprehended. People who had only gotten their atomic toys to play with seventy years previously decided to use them, and almost wiped one another out. That's what the evidence suggests. Simple, provable fact.

The more hypothetical part of the report follows on from that one fact. Millions, even billions of people died in the disaster, yet we know that many were saved. The best and the brightest. Those with the faintest traces of the abilities we would develop in the millennia that followed. With such a concentrated gene pool, those traits just got stronger and stronger. For so long, that has seemed like a good thing, yet now, it seems to have opened us up to the fever. We've run into a genetic dead end that threatens to kill us all. Only by stopping the disaster will we be able to go on.

Do I have the right to do that? Do I have the right to change a whole world?

If not me, then who?

"We're ready, Madame President," Grayson says, coming into the room. "That is, if you still want to go through with it?"

I nod. "We've been through this. I've made my decision. Please just help me to do this."

Grayson nods, leading the way through the White House to the room where he and John have set up the machine. John looks his usual harassed self, a little older than the two of us, flecks of gray starting to show in his hair. He glances up as we arrive.

"Good, you're here. Grayson, have you explained the process?"

He's told me the basics several times, but now, he seems determined to go through it again. Maybe he thinks that it will persuade me not to do it.

"You know that the machine doesn't really move you in time?" he says. "It just disintegrates you, then rebuilds you from scratch in the desired destination."

"That's not a problem, Grayson," I assure him. "Nothing about this is. I've handled wars, rebuilding our country, droughts, hurricanes. Next to those, a little jaunt to stop a bunch of primitive humans from blowing themselves up isn't a big deal."

"It's a *very* big deal, Celes," Grayson insists. "Here, you have knowledge, backup, and technology. There, you won't have any of those things. You'll be a baby, completely helpless."

"You said that I'd have Sara to protect me," I point out. Sara is one of my bodyguards. She was one of the first to make the journey, and one of the strongest. Almost as strong as me.

"We were able to locate Sara because of the signals her powers give off," Grayson agrees. "The machine can track them. In theory, even if she doesn't know exactly who you are, even if she's confused, she should still feel a connection to you and want to protect you. In theory."

"Some days, theory is all that we have," I say. "It's better than having nothing at all."

"You won't have nothing," Grayson promises. "You'll have me."

"No, Grayson. We talked about this. I forbade it."

Grayson shakes his head. "Once you're not here, you can't forbid me anything. I'll go whether you want me to or not."

"You won't remember," I say, trying to reason with him. "You didn't score as well as me on the tests."

"I'll remember," Grayson insists. "I promised Jack I'd look after you, remember? It's been almost four years now, and you know how I feel about you."

"I know," I say. If he's going to admit it, I can. After all, we both know how close we've gotten, "and there's part of me that feels the same way, Grayson, but I have to do this."

He kisses me, and it's such a sweet kiss. Such a gentle kiss. He's kissed me before, a few times, in the years Jack has been gone, when we've both been lonely, or needed it, or just wanted to. With Jack gone so long, expecting to wait would be too much. Yet there's more to this kiss. This is the kind of kiss that promises forever.

"We might not remember each other at first," Grayson promises, "but I'll find you. When I see you, I'll know."

"That's not what the tests say, Grayson."

He shakes his head. "I don't care about the tests. I'll know. I think you will too."

I don't point out the obvious, which is that if I'm in the same time as Jack, Grayson isn't the one my heart will call to, however many intimate moments we've stumbled into over the past few years. There is one other point I can make, though.

"Grayson, you really shouldn't go. You're needed here to fight the disease."

"I'm going after you, Celes," Grayson insists.

I look over at John. "Don't let him go back, John. He isn't to follow unless there's no other way, understood?"

"Celes..." Grayson begins, but I cut him off with a kiss. It might be Jack I'm going after, but that doesn't mean I don't love Grayson at least a little by now. I might have tried to ignore it before, tried to pretend that what was between us wasn't serious, but I guess I can risk it now. After all, I might not be back. So I kiss him. I kiss him in a way that isn't sweet, or gentle. It's just passionate. It's just us.

"I'll be back, Grayson," I say. I laugh. "Thanks to time travel, I'll be back before you even know it." I take a moment to look at the fading machine. It will, technically, kill me. It will scatter my atoms, saving only a plan from which to recreate me at the other end of the wormhole into the past. It is, when I think about it like that, an insane thing to want to do.

For love though, and for the sake of the world, I'll do it.

Celes, Jack, and Grayson's stories continues in

Falling (FADE #2)

Forgotten (FADE #3)

Fever (FADE #4)

Available at all bookstores!

Kailin Gow

A FINAL WORD

Reasons Why?

I get asked this all the time, why do you interact with your readers so much?

1) The answer is simply because I see many of my readers as friends.

I'm a reader, too, and over the years, I've gotten to know some of you through Facebook, Twitter, or even at events I'm participating in. You have read my books, understood the story, and have come to love the characters in these stories as much as I do.

Over the years, I've gotten to know many of my readers. I share your pain when you lose a love one, congratulate you on victories, go through your birthdays and dramas at home and work. So you see, in other words, a lot of my readers have become friends of mine. You read my books, and even understand me like a friend understands a friend.

2) I know how reading can be time-consuming so I am pretty happy when a reader Facebook me and tells me she just read one of my books and she knows she'll be one of my biggest fans. I can't tell you how incredibly touched I am when someone tells me this. It literally brings tears to my eyes.

Not only does this feel incredible, and I am truly honored, but I want my readers to know from the bottom of my heart, this:

3) You Make Me, an Author, feel Warm and Fuzzy, too!

When you love my books and even reach out to me to let me know how much you love my books or that it has touched you in some way, and even write a review about it, you can't imagine how happy that makes me. I'm only human you know. It makes me feel good about what I'm working hard for.

4) My Readers are Not Only Interesting, but they are Fun, Smart, and Great to Hang Out with!

So, please don't be a stranger. Come on by and say "Hi" on Twitter, Facebook, or my blogs. And become a Facebook friend of mine and vice versa. I really do want to find out more about you, and consider it a great honor that you're a reader of mine.

From the bottom of my humble heart:

THANK YOU!

Kailin Gow

You can find me at:

Website: http://www.kailingow.com

Facebook:
http://www.facebook.com/OfficialKailinGow

Instagram:
http://instagram/kailingow

From USA Today Bestselling Author for

Young Adults

Kailin Gow

comes

PULSE

Kailin Gow

17 year-old Kalina didn't know her boyfriend was a
vampire until the night he died of a freak accident. She
didn't know he came from a long line of vampires until
the night she was visited by his half-brothers Jaegar and
Stuart Graystone. There were a lot of secrets her
boyfriend didn't tell her. Now she must discover them
in order to keep alive. But having two half-brothers
vampires around had just gotten interesting···

EXCERPT FROM

PULSE

By Kailin Gow

****

prologue

She ran like an animal. Her clothes were wet, sopping, clinging to her thighs and to her chest, hollow and transparent around the curve of her shoulders. Her hair shook out droplets of rain; her cheeks were flushed and she was breathless. He could see her heartbeat throbbing at the side of her throat, see it in the rhythmic panting, hear it from across the street, pounding in his ears, intermingled with the thunder bolting from the sky. He could feel it – it felt like an earthquake to him, shaking his ribs, his shoulders, his legs. It had been so long since he had seen a heartbeat like hers – since he had felt a heartbeat at all.

The skies had opened up – as they so often did in North California – without any warning, without any hesitation. It was as if the smooth blue glass ceiling of the world had shattered all at once, letting the primordial oceans pound down upon the pavement. He could see her consternation, her irritation – she wanted nothing but to get out of the rain, to dry herself off, to curl up into
something warm and dry.

But Jaegar loved the rain. He loved the energy – the pulse of life beating down upon the earth. He could hear the scattered raindrops in their rhythmic approach to earth and pretend that each fall of rain was a beat of his dead heart. And she was alive with the energy, too – *alive* as he had never seen a woman alive, tossing her hair back, running into shelter, and her lips were pink and her cheeks were red. He remembered that his lips would never again be pink, that his cheeks would never again be red.

She was so young.

Humans so often surprised him in that way. They looked no different from him – he could have been seventeen; he had been seventeen for so long – but their youth never failed to surprise him. The way the world was so new to them – that rain could still take them by surprise, when he had seen so many rainfalls.

He could smell her. The wind carried her scent to him like an animal's scent, and it was all he could do to keep his fangs in check. He leaned heavily upon the branch and parted the leaves to get a better look at her. He could feel the blood – stagnant in his veins – begin something like a torpid, sluggish, shift towards life – the closest thing he would ever get to a heartbeat. She was the sort of girl who made young boys' hearts pound, he thought – and they never knew how lucky they were to experience that sensation.

For it was the physical aspect of it, he thought, that humans understood least of all. They romanticized vampires, of course – how terrible it would be to live at night! To drink blood! To prey upon humans! These were things they could intellectualize, understand. Humans had been forced to commit murder. Humans had been forced to bite back their most natural, primal desires – and so they could almost understand, when they imagined vampires, what it was like to feel that insatiable hunger for a woman's throat, her breast, her wrist. But not a human in the world had ever been alive without *living*, without a heartbeat – and so they took it for granted – what it meant, that constant linear throbbing, clock-like, towards inevitable death. For Jaegar was a vampire, and he was not alive, and the dull ache in his chest where a heartbeat should have been was for him one of the most agonizing things in the world.

They don't know, he thought. *They'll never understand.*

He had been told that she was the one. He

had waited for her until sunset – the sun agonizing upon him, even with the ring around his finger. Vampires were not meant for light, and even the strongest magic could not take away the pain, searing, burning, aching, in his flesh. He was unnatural in sunlight, and only now that dusk was beginning to settle over him could he find relief. He sat perched in the tree, obscured by the leaves, staring at her as she ran down the street.

He leaned in too closely – the birds noticed at last that something was wrong in their midst and took flight; a flurry of wings beat up around him and the branch snapped from the tree and plummeted to the earth below.

It was enough time to make a distraction.

He concentrated, and in half a second he was behind her, so close he could feel the wind blow her hair upon his lips, and then he opened the umbrella above her.

"Miss," he said.

She startled.

"What the..." She rounded on him.

"You looked wet," he said. She did not seem amused.

"I'm warning you," she said. "I know kung fu."

He had learned kung fu once, many centuries ago. He thought it better not to mention it.

"I'm sorry," he said. "I was just trying to help."

She softened.

"Thanks," she said, lamely. "I'm sorry – I didn't mean to snap at you. But you need to learn not to sneak up on people like that. You scared me."

Her eyes remained fixed upon the tree from which he had come. A suspicious glare clouded her gaze. Had she seen – was she wondering? He knew she knew something was wrong. He tried to maintain whatever pleasant normalcy he could. The sequoias were tall, after all. No human could survive a jump from them – he knew she knew this. He knew she thought he was human.

From USA Today Bestselling Author
Kailin Gow

BITTER FROST

All her life, Breena had always dreamed about fairies as
though she lived amongst them... beautiful fairies living
amongst mortals and living in Feyland. In her dreams,
he was always there – the breathtakingly handsome but
dangerous Winter Prince, Kian, who is her intended.
Then she sees Kian, who seems intent on finding her
and carrying her off to Feyland. If she is his intended,
why does he seem to hate her and want her dead? And

her best friend Logan has suddenly become protective.
Things are getting strange...

EXCERPT FROM

BITTER FROST

****

Prologue

The dream had come again, like the sun after a storm. It was the same dream that had come many times before, battering down the doors of my mind night after night since I was a child. It was the sort of dreams all girls dream, I suppose – a dream of mysterious worlds and hidden doorways, of leaves that breathe and make music when they are rustled in the wind, and rivers that bubble and froth with secrets. *Dreams*, my mother always told me, *represent part of our unconsciousness – the place where we store the true parts of our soul, away from the rest of the world.* My mother was an artist; she always thought this way. If it was true, then my true soul was a denizen of this strange and fantastical world. I often felt, in waking hours, that I was in exile, somehow – somehow less myself, less *true*, than I had been in my enchanted slumber. The real world was only a dream, only an echo, and in silent moments throughout the day it would hit me: *I am not at home here.*

I would shake the thought off, of course, dismiss it as stupid, try and apply my mother's armchair psychoanalysis to the situation. But then, before bed, the thought would come to me, trickle through the mire of worries (boys, school, whether or not I'd remembered to charge my IPod before getting into bed, whether or not my banner would be torn down yet again from the homeroom message board) – *will I have the dream tonight?* And then, another thought would come to me alongside it. *Will I be going home again.*

And the night before my sixteenth birthday, the dream came again – stronger and more vivid than it had ever come before, as if the gauzy wisp of a curtain between reality and dream-land had at last been torn open, and I looked upon my fantasy with new eyes.

I was a fairy princess. (When waking, I would chide myself for this fantasy – sixteen-year-old girls should want to start a fruitful career in environmental activism, not twirl around in silk dresses). But I was a fairy princess, and I was a child. I dreamed myself into a palace – with spires reaching up into the sun, so that the rays seemed to pour gold down onto the turrets. The floors were marble; vines bursting with flowers were wrapped around all the colonnades. The halls were covered in mirrors – gold-framed glass after gold-framed glass – and in these hundred kaleidoscopic images I could see my reflection refracted a hundred times.

I was a toddler – perhaps four, maybe five years old, decked out in elaborate jewels, swaddled in lavender silk, yards and yards of the fabric – the color of my eyes. I hated the color of my eyes in real life – their pale color seemed to make me alien and strange – but here, they were beautiful. Here, I was beautiful. Here, I was home.

The music grew louder, and I could hear its melody. It was not like human music – no, not even the most beautiful concertos, most elaborate sonatas. This was the music that humans try to make and fail – the language of the stars as they twinkle, the rhythm of the human heart as it beats, the glimmering harmony of all the planets and all the moons and all the secret melodies of nature. It was a music that haunted me always, whenever I woke up.

Beside me there was a boy – a few years older than I was. I knew his name; somehow my heart had whispered it to my brain. *Kian.* All the palace around me was golden – with peach hues and warm, pulsating life – but Kian was pale, pale like snow. His eyes were icy blue, with just a hint of silver flecked around the irises; his hair was so black that ink itself would drown in it. He seemed out of place in the vernal palace that was my home – out of season with the baskets of ripe fruit that hung down from the ceiling, with the sweet, honey-strong smell of the flowers. But he was beautiful, and all the more beautiful for his strangeness.

We were dancing to the music, our bodies echoing the sounds we heard – or perhaps the sounds were echoing us. We were learning the Equinox Dance. It was the dance that we would dance on our wedding day.

It was a custom in this fairy kingdom that royal children would learn this dance – the most complicated and mysterious of all dances – for their wedding days. And so we all practiced, day after day (night after dream-rich night), for the day that we would come of age, and dance the dance truly, our feet moving in smooth unison, echoing the commingling of our souls.

My father was the fairy king of the Summer Kingdom – a place where everything tasted like honey and felt like the morning sun on your forehead. Kian's mother was the Winter Queen of the Winter Kingdom, a place beyond the mountains where cool breezes turned into arctic chill, where a castle made of amethyst stood upon a rocky peak, and evergreens dotted the horizon. And it was only fitting that our two kingdoms should meet, should join together; we were the chosen ones.

"You will be my Queen," the boy whispered to me. His voice was confident, strong.

The dance was still difficult for us. I got tangled in my waves of lavender satin, tripping over his silver shoes. He in turn kept fumbling with his hands, trying to spin me around the waist and instead, elbowing me in the side – but somehow it didn't hurt.

"Silly," cried the other girl watching us. She, like Kian, was stunning – her hair was as long and lustrous as a starless night; her eyes were silver, like the pelt of a wolf. She was called Shasta, I knew. "Silly – that's not how you dance." She giggled, and her eyes glittered with her laugh.

And then everything changed and became chaos – my home was suddenly ripped apart and replaced by a new scene. Something – *something* – was attacking, something with teeth and horns and claws that ripped, something that made a great and bellowing sound I could hear even when I pressed my hands tightly to my ears. *The Minotaur.*

The screaming came from all directions; everybody was running – me and Shasta and Kian – and the adults, all of them – away from the Minotaur, into each other. Everyone had gone mad. And then someone – someone – was fighting it, a cavalcade of fairy knights each shining in his golden armor – and some knights from the Winter Kingdom too, in their silver.

The Summer King and Queen were there, and the Winter Queen was there too. She looked like Shasta, but older – and her face was different. There was something hard and glinting in her eyes that I could not see in Shasta's, like the shiny specks in stone. I was afraid.

"This is your fault!" a voice snapped – I could not tell to whom it belonged.

"No – it's yours!" Another voice – equally angry, equally cold.

"If it hadn't been for your kingdom..."

"Don't give me those excuses – the Minotaur is a device of your court!"

The voices grew higher and stranger, angrier, louder, quicker and quicker in their retorts until I felt like I was surrounded in a cacophony of rage, bellowing over and over again until at last all I heard was:

"It's all because of that girl!"

And for a moment, they were all silent, and all of them were staring at me.

I could not understand, but it did not matter. Before I could think, could understand what was going on, what was happening to me, the scene had changed again.

I felt his arms around me. That was the first thing; I felt it before I could see anything, see him. I felt his arms encircle my shoulders, feel him brushing my shoulder blades lightly with his fingertips. I shivered. His hands took mine. I could see him. It was Kian, but he was older, now, and so was I – both a young man and a young woman – staring at each other. Age had only made us more beautiful; his hair was longer, now, and his eyes sharper, with greater depth. I could see my reflection in his eyes; my hair was longer too: a deep, warm brown with flecks of gold studded throughout. And I could see my expression – full of fear, full of joy – as he bent down closer to me, as his lips came ever closer to mine.

"Oh, Breena," he said to me. "My Breena."

His blue eyes took on a look of sharp determination; he stared at me with such intensity that I felt that his eyes had penetrated into the truest part of my true soul, a part hidden even to the rest of this strange and wonderful land.

"I will kill you, Breena. It is what I have to do. It is decreed." He cupped my face with his hands, and I could feel his cool breath whispering upon my cheek. "We are mortal enemies."

Always, every night, that same dream – that same fear, that same joy. When I woke up each morning, I felt a profound sense of loss, a yearning that stretched so deeply it crossed the bounds of reality itself. The alarm clock would ring, and everything would change. I was a nearly-sixteen-year-old girl, with suede boots, with T-shirts bearing sayings I believe in." I had an IPod, a cell phone, my laptop (with pages full of html code for my brainchild, teensforgreatergood.com). I spoke in rushed slang about the latest films and television shows, played video games with Logan, teased him when he won, teased him when he lost. I wore little to no makeup and complained about homework during G-Format. The idea of dating – of fumbling high school boys trying to score in between stolen keg stands, of Facebook relationship statuses and hastily-texted endearments – repulsed me.

But for a few hours each night, I was somebody else. I was a princess in a castle, with a dress made of lavender and besides me there is a prince with arctic-blue eyes, and arms wrapped closely around me, and lips coming nightly ever closer to mine...

I was home.

Kailin Gow

Other Books By Kailin Gow

Fantasy Romance Series
<u>FROST SERIES</u>
<u>Age 15 and Up</u>

Bitter Frost and The Wolf Fey
Forever Frost
Silver Frost
Frost Kisses
Midnight Frost
Frost Fire
Spring Frost
Enchanted Frost
Ring of Ice
Ring of Fire
The Fairy Letters

The Wolf Fey: Frost Series Spin-Off
Age 15 and Up

The Wolf Fey
The Red Wolf
Wolf Magic

The Fairy Rose Chronicles
(FROST Series that Takes Place 5 Years Earlier than the Bitter Frost Series)
AGE 9 and Up

The Fairy Rose
Fairy Fair (Fairy Rose Chronicles #2)
Pixies vs. Fairies (Fairy Rose Chronicles #3)

DESIRE
Age 17 and Up

Desire
Summer Wishes
Shattered
Passion

FADE
Age 15 and Up

FADE

Falling
Forgotten
Fever

Wicked Woods Series
Age 15 and Up

Wicked Woods
Shimmer
Silver
Silence
Sight
Shifter

Alchemists Academy Series
Age 13 and Up

Stones to Ashes
Elemental Explosions
The Quantum Games
The Year of the Elite

Wordwick Games Series (An SAT-Prep Series)
Age 15 and Up

Rise of the Fire Tamer
The Ascension
The Return

Want More Edgy books for Teens and Up like this one?

Enter

Sparklesoup Teens

Sparklesoup.com/Teens

Where you will find edgy books for teens, young adults, and new adults that would make your heart pound, your skin crawl, and leave you wanting more...

Feed Your Reading Addiction

FORGOTTEN: FADE Book 3